The

King of Nigh

By the Same Author

The Keeper of Fire
The Mermaid Plight

The Way to Westport

The King of Nigh

Book Two of
The Dolphin Code Trilogy

Davina Marie Liberty

First paperback edition May 2021

Map by Davina Liberty

ISBN 979-8510808612 (paperback)
ASIN : B095XYXY68 (ebook)

www.libertyreads.net

For Grandma Marie

I am truly your descendant

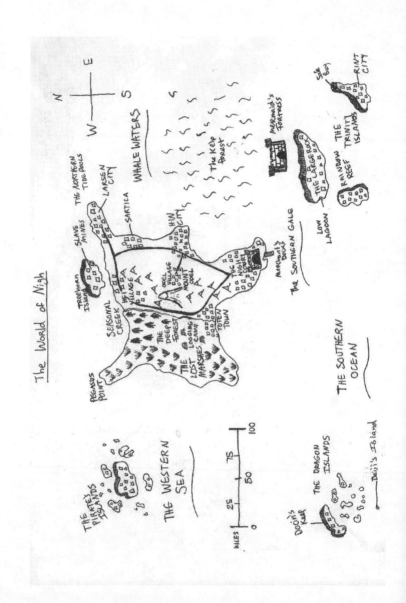

The World of Nigh

Chapter One
The King

THE BOY

Zechi was breathing hard as he fled on foot through the thickness of the trees of the Nigh forest. He leapt nimbly over puddles and fallen logs, and he could hear the beast hot on his heels, panting and snorting loudly.

The boy jumped over a ditch and his leather boots gave a tight squeak as he landed roughly into a crouch, one hand touching the dirt, a full grin on his face. He sprang into the air, his reaching arms finding the rough bark of an overhanging tree branch. The animal passed right beneath his feet.

Zechi pulled himself up and glanced down at the boar, which doubled back. It was squealing and grunting as it dug its tusks into the tree bark in a fit of anger, snorting and wanting nothing more than to

1

gore him. He placed his hands upon the tree trunk and closed his eyes prayerfully.

"*I'm going to need a little help, Sounet,*" Zechi muttered. "*Give me branches to swing upon.*" All at once the trees heeded his request, and across the grove a line of branches creaked as they lowered themselves as far as he could see. He smiled as they stretched out before him and he bent his knees, then leapt!

His leather-bound palms caught onto one tree branch and he swung himself onto the next. He swung back, letting his weight carry him through the air to the next branch, where he teetered precariously and lost his grip.

He nearly cried out but was silent as his hands touched nothing but air, then he hit the ground and rolled up into a crouching position. He drew his knife and looked all around him, his heart pounding furiously. A sore spot on his face twinged painfully and he touched it. His hand came away bloody.

Where was it? He turned in a full circle, slowly and carefully. Then, he heard a light snort behind him. He swung to the left, but it was too late. The pig lunged out from the bushes, running him down. He felt one of its hooves step on his arm as he was trampled, then the knife was knocked from his hand and he swore. He tried to stand as the animal circled back around, but he wasn't quick enough.

Then, a vine moved of its own accord. It swung down to him and the boy caught it with his open fingers. It lifted him into the air, pulled back and flung him forward, and he snatched at the next branch as he fell.

2

"Thank you!" he cried to the trees, laughing, pulling himself onto the branch.

The young boy palmed his way through the trees until he saw a sliver of blue ahead. The boar was still in hot pursuit below, and Zechi whooped with excitement, his powerful arms moving more quickly than his thoughts could keep up with.

The trees thinned out, then opened up to the bay. He let himself fly into the ocean with a splash, ignoring the shock of the cold water. He swam away from the shore a little ways, and looked back, a second knife drawn from his boot, his eyes searching for the boar. The tree line was still.

Zechi smiled, sheathed the blade, and wiped water and blood from his face. The bay of Nigh was wide, and the castle sat along the shore not a boat's length ahead. He treaded water as he checked to see that the little bag of Sapphires he wore around his neck was still accounted for. Satisfied, he began to swim to the castle, but after a few short strokes, a splash in the water nearby caught his eye.

He frowned and peered closer, and a Dolphin surfaced in front of him, sending up a woosh of misty spray. The Dolphin had a quick, keen eye and a strong body. Zechi smiled and was pleased, rather than startled, and he neared his head to the creature and felt the familiar pull into the Dolphin's mind.

"Perhaps you should have left her piglets alone, master Zechi," Arill suggested.

ℶ

THE KING

The King of Nigh stood upon the great stone dais that had served many a king before him. He had since removed the velveteen throne, which did not hold well his Centaur body, and he stood boldly before all who came to beseech him. His horse's body, hair and tail were a deep black that rivaled his eyes, which could sometimes seem fierce.

His shoulders were broad, and a deep scar ran the length of his upper body, from his shoulder to the middle of his chest. It was something of amusement to him to not tell any of the court how such a scar came to be, though it was whispered of amongst the servants and courtiers of the castle. He wore a leather strap across his dark naked body, but the holster for his bow and arrows were empty; he kept only his knife and sword fastened now.

The king's two hired Scribes stood nearby, quills at the ready. There was the human Nia in her usual purple robes, her silver hair and eyes bright and alert. She leaned heavily upon her cane. She was always sneaking out to the garden to smoke from her slender pipe when she thought he wouldn't notice. She had once been the Head Elder of Toten Town, and King Mangiat had taken her under his employ the same day as Gance.

The Elvin Elder Gance was a quiet man, always listening intently to everything anyone ever said. He wore black robes that clasped high to his throat, obscured slightly by his long, yellow hair. His ears were long and pointed, and Mangiat took this as a symbol to Nigh, that he aimed for a diverse counsel from both Man and Mystical worlds. These two stared piercingly at all who entered the Hall, but listened as if they did not quite see or hear those around them.

General Morim stood tall beside him in his red officer's coat with its big brass buttons and white cords. Morim was a loyal man, and Mangiat valued him for that. He had a great understanding of political unfoldings, and Mangiat kept him on as his personal Vizier. The General stood smoothing his bushy brown mustache, keeping a watchful eye over the floor of the Great Hall. He was holding the king's scepter in his fist, noting all that unfolded before them.

The Royal Guard lined the hall's walls in tarnished armor, ready to move at Morim's signal, at any time. They were well-trained men, servants to Nigh.

On this day Mangiat looked out upon several audiences of Man, and he rubbed his temples with stress as they each made their cases before him.

"King Mangiat," one man in tattered peasants' garb began respectfully, sinking deeply into a bow. His hair was grayed and oily, his hands and bare feet calloused and dirty. He was obviously a man of poverty.

"Declare yourself," Mangiat said, not unkindly.

The Scribes' eyes bore into the man, who looked fearful.

"I am Bowen, a Miller in the Odel Village. My wife is of the citizens who took up arms in the Odel Mountain War."

5

"And what is your peace, good sir, my utmost respect and appreciation to your wife and what she has done for our world," Mangiat added, as was the custom. The man hesitated, and Mangiat knew he stared at his scar.

"It is a plea for my friends," he said finally. "The ones who sit in your dungeon at this very moment, awaiting their deaths."

Mangiat's face lost its polite look of focus and became very stern, even angry. "What your friends have done was a pure violation of the Code. This is a shared world we live in, and it is time that your people come to terms with this."

At the raise of the king's voice, his Royal Guard gripped their war axes and tightened their bulky stances, ready to move at his order.

Bowen glared at the king openly now, no longer biting his tongue. "They have done nothing!" he blurted out. "They wanted to log the forest that is now open to us! There is an industry in it, a promise that this world will grow! Can you imagine every Man and Mystic with a job? New homes built? Not of thatch and mud or stone, but of wood? It is a promise that our children's stomachs will be filled! You know as well as anyone that we are jobless, half-starved!"

"They burned her down!" the king roared suddenly, feeling sickened. The Scribes' quills were scribbling furiously.

"They had every right to! We share our schools, our villages and homes with these Mystical creatures! Their holidays, their churches and rituals are blasphemous! There is not enough food or space

6

in our world for us to mingle. Not enough work to keep jewels in our purses! These creatures say that the land is not ours, but it is theirs, and they loan it to us! My friends had every right to protest against such things, no matter how horrible their actions." The corners of Bowen's mouth twitched into a frown and he looked nearly frightened.

"They burned down the Queen of the Forest," Mangiat hissed, "in an act of defiance to their Mystical brethren. There is war because of it! A rift between Man and Mystical peoples where there should have been peace. Your friends will be hanged on charge of murder by the next moon, and unless you tarry to stand with them, I suggest you make your way!" He pointed towards the great door.

"You –" Bowen sputtered, hardly able to find his words. "You are dirt, scum, lower than them!" he shouted, fresh spittle splattering his soiled coat. "A cursed Centaur! You are not a king!" He spat upon the marble floor.

"Guards!" snapped General Morim, unable to accept such rudeness, "take this man away."

"Wait," Mangiat said, holding up one hand. The guards paused, and General Morim respectfully awaited his orders.

"Show mercy to this common man who does not know any better. It is true that there is hardship in the coexistence of Man and Mystical, and there is much that needs adjusting. You there, Bowen." Bowen glared up at his king.

"I may be a lowly Centaur, but I still rule Nigh. Thank you for what you have said this day; it is sure

7

that I will not soon forget it. Go on your way and we will do what we can for our world in these troubled times." He nodded at the guards who escorted the Miller to the door.

As soon as the man had gone, Mangiat brought one hand to his head. His headaches had progressed by far in the last year, but none were so terrible than in this last month. The receiving of the news of Jayna's death had been quite disturbing, and there had been rioting outside the castle for weeks. Zechi had been begging to make a pilgrimage to the site for many days now, which he thought odd, as Zechi had never met Jayna, to his knowledge. Besides, Mangiat was not yet ready.

One year of peace hadn't been all that much, he decided. When he had taken to the throne five years ago it was a happy year, one which he looked back on with many fond memories. Ports of trade had been established between the major coastal cities, and Nigh's economy had seen quite a booming in its exchanges of goods for profit. Mangiat had governed the throne very wisely, and it had been some time before any dissenting voices arose from the newly joined citizens.

"Sire?" General Mormin asked gently, touching his shoulder.

Mangiat jumped, his troubled thoughts interrupted. "Oh. Yes. Let us take a walk, shall we? Circle the court and get some fresh air?"

"Yes, yes," Morim agreed. He held out the king's scepter, which Mangiat refused with the wave of a hand.

"You still find it troublesome?" They both looked down at the jeweled stick and its bronze etching of the Nigh coat of arms, which Mangiat never took to.

He said simply, "I govern the throne, I do what is right for my people, but I will never claim a lineage to it."

They walked down the stone steps into the sunny courtyard, his hooves clattering upon the cobblestones. Mangiat took some deep breaths of the fresh air. How he missed the woods.

"My lord, we must sign the treaty," Morim insisted. "A compromise must be reached. Certain lands will be signed for and permits issued for the logging of charted trees and areas of the woods. It will give Man the wealth he is looking for, and putting restrictions on them will soothe those Mystical creatures angered so."

Mangiat looked to his Vizier sharply. "We log the Deep Forest, then? Do you know that each and every tree has a soul, has a mind? It would be as *murder*."

"It is for the good of many."

Mangiat snorted in contempt, but did not answer. He knew he could not let his own personal bias interfere with the prospect of oncoming war, but he was loathe to set his seal to any such papers.

"Customs are clashing everywhere," Morim went on, as Mangiat paused to brush his fingers over the carefully pruned rose bushes. "Even among our own armies soldiers are having difficulties training together. Man and Centaur and Elf. We are on the brink of another war. It is not well."

The king was silent and he watched a small bird splash about in the stone birdbath. There were the Nigh forest grounds open to him, but they were fenced off, the game released there. It was not natural.

"A ship loaded with goods made passage north, to Treehorn Island, to the miners," Morim continued. "They took a new route, which was assumed to be quicker, crossing the Southern Ocean. The messengers report that they never landed at the docks."

Mangiat gently stepped towards the bird with one outstretched hand and watched it fly away.

"There has also been a severe shortage of jewels. We have doubled the working shifts at the mines, but there simply aren't enough within the rocks. My king, the Mystics most heartily protest against Man's currency. They do not see a need for its use or circulation, and the Elves despise mining it themselves. It has set things most unbalanced. Those Mystics who do adopt it, however, cause its value to be spread so thin throughout the populace that no one can agree to the difference in value between a Ruby and a Pearl! It-"

"I know these troubles," Mangiat interrupted calmly. "I know these woes; they are not new to me." They both looked deeply pensive as they walked through the cobbled court, heads low, hands behind their backs.

Yes, it was true the Elves' hard labor was most unjust in the mining of jewels. And the currency reaped from it was losing value, just as the General said. It was certainly cause for concern, but what was most particularly troubling to him was the lack of Mowat's presence or correspondence at the news of Jayna's death. It was highly unusual for him to remain so silent, Keeper of Life or not.

Mangiat paused on the veranda and looked down upon the cluttered city of Nigh that fanned out below them. How he missed the forest! He turned away.

General Morim and the king made their way back into the Grand Entrance Hall, back to the throne and its stone dais. Mangiat took a deep breath before motioning for his next audience to enter, but a figure sprinting across the grass outside the castle caught his eye.

He looked out the stained-glass window and saw a young boy in his brown clothes running towards the castle door.

"Sire?" General Morim shouldered up next to him.

"My student," he replied with mild interest. "See him in."

₪

Mangiat looked at him with a mixture of pride and exasperation. Zechi had come to him after the Odel Mountain War five years ago when he was nine years old, on the back of General Morim's horse. He was a silent whimpering lad, and it took nearly a year of stern tutelage to get the boy to speak of his own accord.

He could never figure out exactly why Zechi stayed. His parents were alive now, as were all who

11

had passed in that time, but he never went home to Toten Town. He insisted that he was to stay on under the king's very instruction, and this Mangiat allowed him, seeing the boy's willingness and intelligence were so severe.

Zechi was none too tall. His hair was a mousy brown, which he kept short. He usually had a sunburn or scratches on his face, and it was a mystery to all what the boy did with his spare time. Though he could wear a Prince's garments if he chose, he opted for peasant's clothes, claiming them to be more comfortable and practical for his purpose. What that purpose might be, he would never say, and with this he mystified the entire court. The king, though baffled, did his best to give Zechi a proper rearing.

Mangiat had even sent the boy for a year's schooling at the Nigh Academy, where he learned his books and swordplay. He was to return there upon his eighteenth year for further schooling, and the king often wondered what to do with the boy until then.

Zechi burst into the Grand Entrance Hall breathing heavily, his clothes sopping wet, and Nia's lip curled at the pools of water collecting on the marble floor beneath him. His student stood before him now, looking, for the first time in Mangiat's recollection, eager to speak.

"What have you been doing, my friend?" he asked the boy, looking him up and down. He was quite a mess.

"Training," Zechi answered quickly, "but there is that which I wish to say!"

The king nodded, giving him the floor. Zechi paused, as if unsure of what to say first.

"Say on," Mangiat urged.

"It is Mowat. He is missing."

Mangiat stood up straight and lunged forward. "What is this you say?"

"I met Arill in the bay. He says that Mowat disappeared four days ago, with no explanation. He suspects he has been kidnapped!"

Mangiat frowned. "Perhaps you are both mistaken," he said gently. "Mowat has powers far beyond that which you and I understand."

"That is what I said," Zechi insisted, hardly able to contain himself, "but we are both wrong. Mowat relinquished most all of his powers five years ago. He is as any man now."

Both Mangiat and Morim stared, openmouthed. Even Nia and Gance stopped writing for a moment. Mangiat quickly came to his senses. He said, very seriously, "does Arill have any idea of where to look?"

Zechi hesitated again and Mangiat's eyes narrowed. "What is it, boy?"

"There was something he wanted to tell Deiji," he answered softly. "He took a small boat and rowed himself across the sea. Arill traveled alongside him until they were caught in a storm… They were separated and Arill found the boat later. But Mowat wasn't in it."

Mangiat put his hand to his aching head. This could not be.

"Master, Mowat knows nothing of Jayna's death. Arill has requested your assistance."

Mangiat nodded. Mowat was his friend, his Teacher and mentor. He had to find him.

"Sire?" Zechi sought his gaze. How unusual. Zechi was one who avoided eye contact at all costs.

"Yes, say on." He looked awkwardly flustered and he knew it.

"I think we need to start where Arill left off."

"Meaning?" His Centaur's heart sank and rose quickly, a sickening motion.

"We need to speak to Deiji," Zechi said firmly. There was a hollow silence and Mangiat looked away.

"I shall, er, write her a letter then," he said briskly. He rose, nodding his excusal and made his way to a side door and into his private quarters.

ﬥ

He slumped down on his floor-level bedding and eyed his desk and feather quill nervously. "Has it really been five years?" he asked himself with a knot of anxiety in his belly.

He and Deiji had corresponded yearly since her departure, sending their letters across the sea with Polk, her beloved falcon. They never spoke of their love, yet Mangiat's feelings had not faded, and he found himself longing for her at the oddest of times.

After the Odel Mountain War, after Relant's spell had been broken, those wrongly dead had risen and life was pure once more. Mangiat himself had been released of his servitude to Jayna, now that his father was avenged. He had been placed in this position on the throne the day that Deiji was to

14

choose her own destiny. He had been quite sure that Deiji was going to choose him as she stood on the stone dais, but he had been mistaken. She had chosen her Island, and this he did not begrudge, but it did rather confuse him. Or, perhaps, disappointed him. And she gave the throne to him. Now he was king. It was not bad, he decided; it was a matter of principle to lead both Man and Mystical people together in fulfillment of the prophecy. Yet he was stressed.

Mangiat looked out the window. Twilight was falling over the city. He glanced back to his desk again with mounting apprehension. The stars began to show themselves, one by one, and he could all but read an unsettling future for his world there, the same future he saw each and every night. "It may rain soon," he whispered, thinking of spring, reading the whisper of hope. He tore his eyes away.

"Zechi, a word!" he shouted into the doorway, and the boy came running.

"Yes?" he asked eagerly, and Mangiat was taken aback at this sudden show of interest.

"Find Polk for me," he commanded. "It is time to send a message."

Zechi bowed briefly and hurried from the room. Mangiat sighed and turned to his wooden desk.

Chapter Two
The Island

TWO DAYS LATER...

THE KEEPER OF FIRE

A brown haired girl sat astride a large horse as she made her way through the overgrown jungle. Her sword was drawn, her fingers wrapped tightly around its dragon-emblazoned handle. The other held a fistful of snow white mane, and she used the sword to hack at the damp foliage as they trotted in the afternoon sun.

A shadow crossed over the forest canopy and Deiji could see it flicker across the path before them. She kept her eyes to the trail. A dark hole was visible through the brush, and Deiji leaned forward, feeling the strong muscles of the horse's back beneath her. They broke into a gallop just before the ground dipped low into a black, rocky cave and they rode down into it. It was much cooler here, and her horse's hooves echoed throughout the cavern.

"Come on, Puff Puff!" she urged the mare, and she hugged her thighs into the horse's bare back to keep her seat as they sped up. The cave ahead broke into three underground tunnels, and she steered Puff to the left. After five years on the Island, Deiji had thoroughly explored every inch of it. This place was more home to her than any she had ever known, and she knew it well.

It was sunny, hot and humid always, unless a storm blew through. The jungle was full of noisy and colorful creatures, such as she had never seen in all the world. And Deiji had seen her world.

Fragments of rocks and rubble lay strewn before her, blocking parts of her path. She released one hand from the horse's mane and pointed her open hand at the obstructions. Shouting *"Ciechi!"* she blasted them aside without pausing.

The tunnel split again, this time into two, and she continued to the left. She knew that the right would take her directly to the cave, but she wanted to meet Geo and the sky.

A steady incline began and she passed a familiar pillared rock formation before emerging into sunlight once more. The shadow slung low from above, and this time she looked skyward. Her horse reared up and she raised her sword to the clouds.

"To Geo!" she shouted to her Dragon, who swooped down in a circle and made to land beside the trail. Deiji raced beneath him and pulled the white mare into a skid. She dismounted quickly and turned to Geo.

Geo was large, with scales as green as Emeralds. He had frightening poisonous talons and a sharp, spiked tail. His face was very kind and sincere, but if he bared his teeth even the bravest man would whimper.

They walked alongside one another to the cave, which was only around the next bend. They bowed deeply to one another, girl and Dragon, then looked to the sky.

"We honor Geo's beloved mother on this estimated anniversary of her death," Deiji said boldly. "And we wish her hopes in the Timeless Sky where she now dwells. To Geo!" She raised her sword into the sky once more in jubilation.

Geo lowered his head to the mouth of the cave and blew a small stream of green fire onto a single flower. Deiji watched, enchanted, as a bed of colorful flowers began to grow and spread across the path. She glanced into the cave, where the skeleton used to lay.

Geo's mother had been brought back to life, as all were who had died of the fever, which Deiji had relinquished. She had since abandoned her Keep, or had died, perhaps. Her fate remained unknown. Their ceremony now was not that of mourning, for they had not known her, but it was of respect, as one does for a Dragon who has lost their Keep.

They stepped into the cave and reverently added one small treasure to the pile that towered high above them. It was quite a mountain of treasure, and they sometimes helped themselves to it, though they still made a yearly offering – a nicely smoothed stone from the beach, or a pearlescent shell to add to the Dragon's life's collection. When Deiji had first dug through the treasure, which, after all, belonged to Geo in his mother's passing, she was quite surprised as to its contents. Aside from gold and a surplus of jewels, they had also come across goods and other items that Deiji used to furnish the cave she now called home.

The most intriguing had been the books. They were old, delicate things, bound in faded leather with titles like *"Runes in Translation,"* and *"The Dragon."* There was a water-stained paper flap inside one that had three full-scale completed maps of the world. Deiji had been ecstatic, and poured over their pages slavishly until she memorized every corner of the Nigh world.

Also among the dozen printed works had been one fat one, entitled *"The Keeper's Magic."* It had been stored inside a locked chest among other treasure, and Deiji had salvaged it. Thinking it was about Mowat's abilities, she had been shocked to discover it was a volume of evil magic and its practical purposes. But still she read it, kept it, as she had retained and devoured every other book she came across during her extended solitude.

She looked at her friend Geo and smiled in the twinkling lights of the treasure and Dragon Stone on the walls. "Let's go home," she suggested, and he nodded, yawning.

"Puff Puff, disappear until I call for you," Deiji commanded, and the white mare evaporated into mist, without stopping to change back into her true form.

Puff Puff was a form of Djin – a shapeshifting cat of a magical breed. Immortal, and bound to Deiji as her Master, she was obedient to anything the girl asked of her. She was a proper, finicky little cat, and a source of endless amusement to Deiji. She was also a true friend – despite her constant self-centeredness.

Puff Puff could retain any form she requested. Deiji had even figured a way to join with her pet, and thus change her own shape at will.

The girl vaulted onto her Dragon's back and they lifted into the air easily. They rose up and over the jungle, then flew to the beach, to the cliff face that Deiji called home.

Her powers and magical abilities had become much more honed over the years, and each and every day she found herself learning new things. Although she was not nearly perfected in her new position, Deiji still found it in herself to mold the very rock of the cliff by simply willing it to be so.

The cliff face was over one hundred feet high, and it was a sheer drop for the most part, though it fanned out overhead near the top. The mouth to Deiji's cave sat right in the middle. It would be a feat to climb without magical aid.

They flew through the open mouth into a multi-chambered cave that had holes for windows and manipulated stone for furnishings. Her books sat on a high shelf, neatly stacked beside one another. The ornate locked box she had taken from the Keep lay below it, its treasure long since discovered, its lock repaired. She kept the original contents in it untouched, save for the book.

There were silks over the windows, and even a jade statue of a Dragon that she couldn't bear to leave behind, and it guarded her doorpost proudly.

Deiji sighed, grateful to be home. She was quite weary of the jungle today, and had heard the trees whispering, calling to her, which meant that Zechi sought her attention. While she had no qualms against the boy, she knew that he was placed directly under Mangiat, and it was an uncomfortable relationship.

She had never forgotten the kindness and friendship the Centaur had offered, and she was quite keen to take it, only she knew it was not yet the time. She was glad to have spent these last few years in her quiet solitude, studying her books and pondering in only the way that the silent can ponder. It was true that at times she did long for companionship and conversation, but she had Geo and the Puff, and trained with them daily.

She flopped down into a cupped rock, smoothed and covered in thick moss, better than any chair she had sat in on the mainland. She opened *"Ocean Winds and Patterns,"* sipping cool spring water from a golden jewel-encrusted goblet as she settled in.

Geo dozed beside her peacefully. She smiled over her book as he twitched a little, lost in his dreams. The cave was silent, with only the distant roar of the wind on the ocean and the Dragon's slight snores.

She had scarcely read a page when she heard a rustle of wings and sensed a presence approaching her cave. Her heart did a flip-flop. She knew it was Polk, and she set down her mug and book promptly.

She had rescued Polk as a foundling, when he had fallen out of his nest. She cared for him until he could fly, and they always remained friends. His brown feathers and sharp curved beak were pleasant and familiar for her to see, and she found some pride in his healthy looks. He was very loyal and it was not a care to him to pass these messages between her and the king.

Deiji moved quickly to the mouth of the cave to receive her friend on her outstretched arm. There was something odd about this correspondence. Mangiat was quite prompt in writing her a single letter each and every year. This year she had received two already – the usual one, and the last one being less than a week ago, bearing the news that Jayna had been murdered. Though she enjoyed his letters greatly, she knew with a cold feeling in the pit of her stomach that this too was out of the ordinary.

"Hello, Polk!" Deiji called out, and she managed to sound cheery. "You must be exhausted! That's what, five trips in two months?" She stroked the Falcon's feathered breast, and he ruffled his feathers and gave her a piercing stare that showed his agreement.

"Yes, yes, I know, soon to be six." She laughed. "I was not expecting you," she admitted, "but let me see if I can find you a mouse. Puff!"

The cat appeared with a burst of cloud. "Yes?" Puff eyed the Falcon mischievously.

"Please obtain a mouse for our guest. And leave him be, okay? He is not for food," Deiji added strictly.

"Can I play with it?" the little cat asked imploringly. "I mean, just a little?" She swiped one clawed paw in Polk's direction. It was always a true test for Deiji to ignore Puff's alluring gaze, but she shook her head firmly.

"No."

Puff rolled her kitty eyes and Polk fluttered onto the wooden perch that was mounted on the cave wall. Deiji untied the vial from his leg. She unraveled the scroll, her heart beating. The message was short.

"Jai," it began in its usual fashion, referring to her given name, *"Things are not quite so well, but it is beside that of politics and leadership.*

Arill has brought to us the most disturbing news: Mowat is missing. Whether he is dead or has been kidnapped, we do not know, but Arill suspects something of foul nature.

Mowat was on his way to see you – there was that which he wished to tell you in person, but he did not make it.

I request an audience with you at your earliest convenience, though I must say, time is of the essence. Any information you might volunteer would be very helpful.

We will speak shortly.

Mangiat."

She read through it twice, her eyes scanning quickly. A quiet anger sparked at the possibilities of

Mowat being in danger, and a cold rain began to fall from the clouds.

"Geo, wake up," she said firmly, and the Dragon opened his eyes warily.

"Polk? Are you ready to fly? Puff?" She looked at the two, who were deep in a meal of mice, and they both nodded. Geo cocked his head inquisitively. Deiji tried to smile at him, but her lips quivered.

"It looks... It looks as though we are to leave the Island."

ℼ

As they rose above the Island, Deiji turned back to see her home. She brushed her fingers across the horizon and shouted, *"Maeim!"* and fog clouded from her fingertips and settled on the still waters. It spread about the Island, enshrouding it in a thick hanging mist, which she hoped would hide it from all eyes. Not that it mattered; aside from Polk there hadn't been a single visiting soul in all the time that she had lived there.

She found herself looking back, over and over, until it was nothing more than a speck on the horizon, then disappeared.

Deiji hadn't left in five years.

Polk flew alongside Geo, and Puff floated lazily along upon a cloud, licking her coat vainly and keeping pace with absolutely no effort.

It was a full day before they reached Nigh.

Chapter Three
The Journey

THE BOY

$\mathscr{Z}$echi was packing his leather satchel feverishly, checking and double checking that he had all of his knives and his blanket roll. "Extra socks," he muttered to himself, turning to his armoire.

He had his room decorated in earthen colors – bold browns and greens – and he had even coaxed a vine of ivy to creep in through his window and branch out across the stone walls.

His walls looked more like a soldier's than a royal's – knives and daggers hung on display beside his swords. His drawers were full of small items for travel: bandages, miniature cooking tools and rations. He was keenly aware of the stable cellars that held all of the soldiers' supplies, which he pilfered as he was able.

Zechi set his pack by the door leading into the marble entrance hall and loitered about the doorway impatiently. He glanced at the sky. It was a gray day. The weather had been colder these last three nights, and this only fueled his restlessness further. He leaned against the archway and could hear General Morim and Mangiat talking heatedly in the garden court about Arill's information.

"I say he is dead! If Mowat disappeared from his boat, then it is sure!"

Zechi peeked around the corner. He was not the only one eavesdropping. Nia and Gance were crouched behind the shrubbery, leaves in their hair, listening to every word.

Gance was an Elf, and the boy knew little of him. He was quite tall, his light hair very long. Zechi liked his ears, but he was skeptical of the character of the man. He knew for certain that he did not like Nia, who had been the head Elder in Toten Town when he was a child. She sat there, wrapped in her purple shawl and leaning on her cane, the frown she wore every day looking somehow meaner.

The king frowned and shook his head at Morim. "Arill is right. There's something more to this. It's too... unlike him."

"There is much more to think about right now. We sit on the edge of revolution! Mowat is mortal now!" the General argued, and Zechi shrunk away from his angry face. "There is every reason to believe he simply drowned."

"Arill said that Mowat has a history with the sea. The one ability that Mowat retained was to breathe and live underwater, even though he gave that power to Deiji long ago."

They fell silent, and even Zechi found himself doting upon the thought of the girl and her legendary days as a Mermaid.

"Okay," General Morim said finally. "Then what do we do?"

"Wait for Deiji," Mangiat said calmly. "She will know the first step."

"Do you really think you will leave to search for him? I fear for your safety, as well as Zechi's."

"The boy is not coming with me. Deiji and I will travel alongside Arill. You are to watch over the throne and my student while I am away. I will call a meeting for council when she arrives and we will discuss the details then."

Zechi's heart was hollow, and he snatched up his satchel and shouted out, "I will not stay!" He rushed over the threshold and approached them stoutly. Morim looked surprised, but Mangiat did not.

"I am going with you!"

"Calm yourself, boy!" his teacher hissed. "You are to stay here under the General."

"I am meant to go!"

"Zechi." The king's face was soft and serious, and Zechi's hopes fell. He knew by his tone that there was no sense in argument.

"Zechi, as your king, your mentor and your friend, I beg you to remain here and be obedient to my wishes. It is far too dangerous."

"You could use me," he insisted. "I am strong, alert, I —"

Mangiat held up one hand. "No."

Zechi opened his mouth to reply, but he silenced himself. Instead, he glanced to Nia and Gance who hid and said, "well, I notice things that you do not, anyhow," and he nodded towards the bushes.

Morim looked to him in amazement, then at the hedges as he walked back into his room. Zechi could hear the scuffle as he shut the door, but he ignored it, setting his pack right next to the threshold again.

ת

THE KING

Mangiat rubbed his aching temples and prayed for the pounding in his head to subside. Zechi was the closest thing he had ever known for a son, and he guarded the boy both jealously and proudly. He knew he couldn't forgive himself if Zechi were to be injured or worse.

Deiji would know the answers. There was comfort in this thought. More than two hundred and forty-four years had passed since Man rose from the sea, the remnants of dying Mermaids. More than two hundred years since the legendary days of Mowat. Now there was a new force in the world. A new *Jai*.

He sighed again and saw a shadow cross over the courtyard. Snapping to attention, he rose to his feet and galloped out into the mild sunshine, eyes to the sky.

There she was! His heart gave a great leap as the dark haired girl spiraled down atop her forest-green

28

Dragon and into his path. She was wind-blown and tired, but her eyes and smile were still bright, and Mangiat grinned nervously.

She was as tall and willowy as he remembered, though her skin was darker. Her eyes were nearly all black, but looked to be filled with stars, and he stood in awe of this, unable to speak. Deiji smiled. She had a very bright smile.

A soft blue sari was draped loosely around her thin body, and her feet were bare. She hopped down from Geo's back and Mangiat moved as though to hug her, but hesitated. He compensated by placing one hand on her shoulder instead.

"Jai," he whispered, smiling.

"My lord." She bowed. He noticed the familiar sword slung across her shoulders, and he eyed the medallion. It was Deiji!

Zechi came running across the courtyard excitedly. "Milady!" he called out, dropping to one knee and bowing his head.

"Oh, Zechi!" she exclaimed with delight, and she pulled him to his feet and into a tight embrace. The boy looked stunned, but said nothing.

Mangiat cleared his throat. "Zechi, the Lady is tired and needs to rest. Libations, perhaps? A little hot food?" He turned to the girl with question.

"Oh, no," she dismissed him casually. "I am fine." She glanced at Geo, who shrugged a bit.

"Zechi, take Geo to the corral and water him from the horse's trough."

Zechi obeyed the king's order, and they watched him walk alongside Geo, talking animatedly.

"The boy has changed," Deiji said thoughtfully.

29

"Yes, yes," Mangiat agreed, "but it is a very recent change. When he found out about Mowat, he suddenly became very… very passionate."

"Where is Arill?" Deiji asked abruptly. "We should get to work right away."

"Oh. Right. Let us walk to the bay, shall we?" He offered his arm like a proper gentleman. She laughed, but took it.

He escorted her quickly onto the castle grounds and along the fringes of the Nigh forest, and they spoke.

"How have you been?" she asked him pointedly, and with such concern that the king felt as though he might collapse. He slumped, then poured out his thoughts to her, his stress and fears with the new developments concerning Nigh.

"I do not know what must be done," he admitted when he was finished. It was a relief to see her again, to speak to her, to touch...

She looked at him curiously. "It is a strange thing, but I feel as though I know what could be the way to solve all of this, only I cannot place it."

"You may very well know the answer," he said thoughtfully, stopping them so he could face her. He touched her shoulder yet again.

"You do know what you are," he said gently.

"The Keeper of Fire," Deiji said, blushing a little and looking away.

Mangiat nodded encouragingly. "Soon to be the fully endowed Keeper of Life. You are only beginning to understand your full potential, my friend. Arill has been quite adamant about that fact, as Zechi tells me. It is as Mowat intended. Deep inside your mind it is quite probable that you already know the decisions to be made." He caught her gaze and looked full into her large, beautiful eyes. "You need only to unlock such power."

They stared into each other's faces for a moment, then both looked away. The beauty and the awkwardness of the moment did not escape either of them. They continued their walk to the bay, and already Deiji's necklace was glowing brightly in a swirl of jeweled color, as it always did when she was near Arill.

Mangiat watched as his friend plunged into the water without hesitation, calling out the Dolphin's name with obvious enthusiasm. He noticed that once she was submerged she turned into a Mermaid, and the two did not have to touch to speak. He could only hear snatches of conversation from Deiji's end, and only when she raised her head up from the water, at that.

As the minutes passed, he grew fidgety and wanted to join them, but was leery of the water. It was not of his element. He looked out at the bay, which was a large scoop off the shore on the edge of the castle grounds. Further down the shore he could see the faint outline of Merchant's docks and ships being loaded with precious cargo. The spot had been chosen for its moderate depths and calm waters, just one of many developments he himself had been the forerunner of.

After a time the two friends in the bay parted ways, and Deiji came from the waters grinning, her hair dripping, her sari wetted and clinging to her body. The joy of the moment faded a little, and he could tell she was troubled.

"It has indeed passed as Zechi said," Deiji confirmed. "I wonder what it is that Mowat was so set on telling me. He did not tell Arill. Come," she said, and Mangiat looked at her, surprised. "We have devised a plan. Let us speak to your people."

₪

That evening, after the sun had set and all were fed and settled in, Mangiat held meeting in his private hall for consultations. Eight candles burned in the holders on the stone walls.

Around the long table sat the king, Jai, General Morim, and the two most honored Elders in the Nigh City – the two who served as Scribes and as the voice of the common people: Gance and Nia.

He noticed Deiji's surprise when her eyes fell upon the smug-looking silver haired woman, though she was quick to disguise it. Jai was now staring vacantly at a woolen tapestry that portrayed a picture of the woods.

"So what is the course of action to be taken?" Gance asked his king, peering at him closely. His narrow back was straight, his light yellow hair falling loosely behind him.

Mangiat cleared his throat. "Jai and I have spoken, and we have also been to see Arill. We leave tomorrow by the first light of dawn."

"And where will you go?" Morim asked in surprise.

Mangiat opened his mouth to speak, then shut it quickly, turning pale. He was afraid to say it and thus make it true. Deiji said loudly in his stead, "we will first follow the route across the sea, the route that Mowat took. We will see if we can find him there." She rested her elbows casually upon the oaken table, despite the glances and glares of the Scribes. Mangiat smiled.

"And is it well that you be apart from your physician?" Morim asked him plainly, and Mangiat knew Deiji stared at him.

"I will be fine," he insisted.

"And what of Nigh? What will the great city be without its king?" Gance spat skeptically. Nia intertwined her slender fingers and rested them beneath her chin.

"I will leave the throne under the steward of General Morim. If anything should happen to me along the way, I have left written instructions for the care of Nigh in the case of a long-term or permanent absence."

He glanced at Deiji, who was looking to the arched doorway. He followed her gaze and saw Zechi peeking out from the shadows, listening to every word.

"Send that small dog on his way!" Nia blurted out, looking over her shoulder.

"General Morim," Mangiat stated loudly and deliberately, "will also watch over Zechi in my absence. Keep him busy with his books, my friend."

Zechi did not leave, but rather stood quite openly on the threshold.

"What about Nigh's current state? You cannot abandon your kingdom in the midst of such troubles," the elderly Nia said. Her silver hair was quite stunning, her body withered and frail.

"I am not abandoning anything," he answered sharply. He forced himself to meet her gray eyes and hold them there. "Nigh will wait. These troubles are the same as they ever were. Do you understand?" He knew he could not wholly trust these two.

"Yes, my king." She lowered her gaze to the table. He looked around and addressed them all.

"There is but one thing I must declare in my absence: No papers nor treaties will be signed for or agreed upon. I am placing a hold on all of the transactions and taxes from profits of trade in all of Nigh. There will be no war declared and no profit made in light of my absence. Is this clear?" He looked into each of their faces sternly.

"Yes, my king." General Morim bowed.

"Please see to it that the people still make their pleas to the throne. Continue in your act as Scribes and record all such interactions so that I might review them upon my return."

"And how will you travel?" the General asked with concern.

"By boat," he answered promptly, his stomach queasy just thinking about it.

"But where will you find such a boat?" exclaimed Nia. "Nigh has no such vessel to spare!"

He frowned, for he had not thought that far ahead.

Deiji cleared her throat and they all stared at her as she sat bent over the table toying with her amulet.

"I believe I know where to find such a ship," she said slyly.

₪

That night when Mangiat retired to his private quarters his shoulders shook in apprehension. He sat at his desk, eagerly this time, to jot down the days' events in his journal. His mind wandered to Deiji and he sighed some. He finished his entry briskly.

And what of myself and Jai? Having her near me again is by far the most frustrating and wonderful experience. I saw her at the council tonight, looking astounded as I spoke with such authority. I suppose we have both changed some. She herself is more wild than I remember.

I wonder if my fear of water will bring a damper on our journey together?

Chapter Four
The Ship

*D*awn seemed to come early and the fog sat heavy and still on the bay. Shuddering at its clamminess, Mangiat drew his cloak tightly across his shoulders and glanced out the castle window into the bay and shuddered again.

He lifted his black leather satchel and tucked his journal safely inside before adding a set of fresh quills. He left the castle quietly and made for the docks.

A small band of well-wishers had gathered to see them off, including General Morim and Zechi. Mangiat eyed the boy suspiciously and nodded in approval when Morim placed one authoritative hand on Zechi's shoulder, which was promptly shrugged off.

The king looked ahead to his fellow travelers who waited by the waterside. Deiji and Geo both looked eager to go about with the day's unfoldings. Arill splashed about in the bay apprehensively.

He smiled at the group nervously and glanced around, pacing back and forth. He noticed himself pawing at the ground and stopped.

"Where's the ship, Jai?"

Deiji smiled at him, turned to the water, and called forth, "Puff Puff!"

A little cat of wispy cloud appeared at her feet, examining her tiny claws vainly. She sighed and began to smooth the fur around each claw with her little tongue.

"Puff," the girl rebuked sternly.

"I'm Puff Puff!" the cat called out with pride, suddenly excited.

The girl closed her eyes serenely. "Puff Puff, I want you to make us a ship – a good sailing ship of fine wood. She should have at least two masts and tall sails."

As she spoke, those around her gasped, for it seemed as though whatever Deiji saw in her mind, Puff was becoming it now. Puff grew from her little kitty form and stretched out into the shape of a hull, and longer.

She grew larger also, floating out into the bay, and two masts grew towards the sky, wispy sails of cloud attaching themselves to them. Underneath the bowsprit a figurehead formed – an oaken carving of a cat. Across the bow the words *The Princess Puff Puff* appeared, and both Mangiat and Deiji rolled their eyes. The gathering gawked, for never had there been such a ship in Nigh.

They all stared into the bay at this growing spectacle, and Mangiat finally asked nervously, "we don't have to, er, swim out there, do we?"

"Oh, no," Deiji answered hastily, and, "Puff, a lifeboat please!" A small pleasure craft rose from the waves, bumped onto the shore and settled there.

Mangiat looked out at the magnificent ship that sat waiting for them in the distance. He breathed heavily and turned to the spectators. He passed a stern eye over his Scribes, then looked to the General.

"Morim." He nodded to his friend respectfully, then glanced down at his student. "Zechi, look to General Morim in all things. Stay safe, lad." He placed his hand on the boy's shoulder, his throat suddenly tight and he could say no more.

Deiji mounted her Dragon while Mangiat clambered clumsily into the lifeboat. He watched as she rose into the air and shouted "*Azioni!*" and a soft blue light grew from her fingertips and pushed Mangiat's boat across the water ahead of her.

"Oh!" he said in surprise as he glided rapidly across the choppy waves. He grabbed onto the side of the boat and looked back to the shore, and the great castle of Nigh that loomed above them. He closed his eyes to a dull ache and felt a sorrowful longing for the woods, and his old home among the trees.

There was a slight bump and his boat had touched the ship. He looked skeptically up at its wooden hull and the flimsy rope ladder that led to the deck. "And how, exactly, am I to get up there?" he asked sourly to no one.

Deiji popped her head over the rail, startling him. "Geo will help you."

And so Mangiat found himself submitting his weight to the Dragon, who gently closed his massive talons around his horse-like midsection and lifted him onto the deck of the ship.

Suddenly Mangiat felt as if his hooves were completely unsteady! He fell from side to side, attempting to catch himself and find his balance, but the ships' rocking was incessant. His hooves crossed over as he danced across the deck sideways.

Deiji began to laugh. He clung to the main mast and glared at his friend scornfully. "This is funny, is it?"

She laughed loudly, her head thrown back to the sky. "Yes!"

He smiled at little, fairly exasperated. "And why do you not fall over, Jai? How do you stand?" He eyed her two legs with doubt.

"You just feel the sway of the ship and you step with it. Root your hooves to the rock of the waves." She hopped up onto the deck railing and walked across it, her arms out for balance. She laughed again and hopped out onto the trailing ratlines.

He stared. "Right."

She left him to it and proceeded to examine the ship. "Puff Puff, prepare to cast off!" she commanded.

Puff, as the ship, obediently tightened the necessary ropes and lines, and loosened the sails. "We have no wind, my master." Mangiat could not see where her voice was coming from. He watched, fascinated, as Deiji raised her hands to the sky and called upon the Sties, the people of the wind, who lived above the clouds.

"Sties, *Betep!*" she cried, and a strong wind blew. The sails filled, puffed out and they were on their way.

ℼ

"You have learned much," Mangiat said with admiration. He tried to catch her eye. Deiji was hanging onto the rail near the bowsprit, eagerly watching the water rush beneath them. She flashed him a sweet smile.

"Thank you."

He glanced up at Geo, who was clinging to the shrouds behind them, scanning the open sea. It was windy now, and the air was salty and wet. The sun was setting. "Ahoy, Geo!" he called up, speaking loudly over the roar of the wind. He was shivering. Looking about for a distraction, his eyes fell on Deiji. "Where did you learn about boats?" He asked, speaking as one speaks when trying to keep warm; distracted and squirming about.

"I found books in the Dragon's Keep on my Island. One of them was called *'Great Pirates of the Western Sea.'* I read it, and Puff and I have done some training together. The more acute abilities are gained through study and experience. You taught me that."

They leaned over the rail to glimpse Arill keeping pace with the ship, and Mangiat pulled back, sickened by the sight of the rushing water. He watched her dark hair flutter about freely in the wild wind, and her voice interrupted his thoughts.

"We're completely past the Southern Peninsula," she called out. "We should reach the place where Mowat was last seen by morning. I think we can call it a day."

"Then I shall retire." He looked around. "Where to?"

"Would you like the Captain's quarters?" she offered generously.

"Oh, no. You are more Captain than I. Where else is there?"

"The forecastle. Crew's quarters," she explained, when he looked puzzled. "Follow me. Geo will sleep on the deck, on watch."

He obediently trailed after her as she led him down a small hallway past the privy. It opened into a dimly lit square room. The floor was bare, wooden, and a few hammocks of torn canvas hung limply. The room had a strange musty odor that Mangiat couldn't quite place.

Something small skittered across the floor, and Mangiat drew himself back, clutching his leather satchel close to his body.

"On second thought…" he began, and Deiji laughed.

"Come with me."

He followed her across the deck to the opposite side of the ship. She opened the lightweight wooden door and Mangiat felt as though he could breathe again.

There were clean red carpets and moderate works of art on the walls. The bed in the bedroom

41

was too high for his liking, but there were some cushions on the ornate sofa in the sitting room that looked promising.

"If you take the bedroom, I can sleep here," he offered, trying to escape the flush that spread across his face.

"That sounds fine." She touched his arm affectionately, retreated into the bedroom and closed the door.

Mangiat sighed with some sort of relief he could not explain, and set his things down. There was a small porthole beside a low table, and he could see the stars beginning to come out.

"Nigh sits safely for the time... The great city waits," he whispered, and he turned away, looking to put his attention to something else, anything else.

He spied the desk and eagerly took out his journal and quills. He relaxed as he settled in and began to write in his old, familiar fashion.

ꭹ

He woke with his usual dull ache to the rocking of the ship, feeling quite queasy and not at all himself. He wanted a hot cup of tea more than anything.

The door to the bedroom was open and Deiji was nowhere to be seen. His stomach grumbled and he suddenly thought of something. He hurried out onto the deck.

"Jai?" he called out, but there was no answer, save for the ship's creaking. "Geo?" Nothing. He hesitated. "Puff Puff?"

"Hello there, Sir Mangiat," the squeaky little voiced cooed promptly.

"Hello, Puff. Where is Jai?"

"Oh, I do know the answer for that one! But you must give me something in return!"

He was startled. "And what is that?" What could she possibly want of him?

"Tell me I'm pretty." Her voice was silky, coquettish.

"You're very pretty. Now where is she?"

"Aw," the cat actually sounded disappointed. "Say it with *meaning*. Tell me I'm the most beautiful Djin you've ever met."

"You're the *only* Djin I've ever met," he snapped in frustration.

"Very well. They are near the bow."

Mangiat trotted to the front of the ship as best as he was able, to where Geo and Deiji were staring out into the open sea. He stepped up beside them.

"Good morning." He cleared his throat.

"Good morning," Deiji answered easily. She was looking through a small folding telescope. Geo snorted in greeting.

"Jai, I was wondering what we are to do about food. We did not think to pack rations."

"Oh, it is already done. There is food prepared in the galley."

He stared at her blankly.

"In that room over there!" she cried, exasperated. "Go explore the ship or something. Figure it out!" Thunder clapped overhead and he winced. Feeling a tad wounded, he turned to wander off but decided to wait.

"What are we looking for?" He cleared his throat again, wanting to redeem himself.

"We are very near to the closest approximate location that Mowat disappeared. Arill and I are going to explore."

"Explore? You mean to dive under?"

"Yes. You stay with Geo and the ship. Have something to eat while you wait. Ah, we're here." She folded up the telescope and handed it to him. "Puff, cast the anchor!"

She stepped up onto the railing and Mangiat felt his heart quicken in fear. "Be careful!" he blurted out.

Deiji grinned back at him. "Always." She dove headfirst and sank under the waves with a splash. He watched until the ripples faded, then turned to the Dragon.

"Shall we?"

Geo shrugged and followed him as he wandered around the deck. He saw a low-rise archway and went through its open door. It seemed to be a small kitchen of sorts, with a small cast iron stove and racks of tin plates and cooking utensils on a coarse countertop. The room was exceedingly tiny, the wood rough and splintered. He shook his head.

The Dragon could only go so far in as his shoulders, and he watched as Mangiat approached the pot that was still steaming on the flame. He opened its lid and recoiled instantly. It was full of a colorless cornmeal of some sort, still steaming and molded to the pot. He dropped the lid back on and put his head into his hands.

ſ₪

THE KEEPER OF FIRE

Deiji transformed into a Mermaid the moment she touched the water. She laughed a tinkling Mermaid laugh and stretched her long, green tail. She loved being a Mermaid! Arill swam up to her and they danced together, spinning about, rejoicing in the water that was theirs. She grinned sheepishly. It was difficult to escape the Mermaid's natural urges, which were of uncontrollable cheerfulness to be in the water. After they settled down some, she asked, "is this where you last saw him?"

"Yes," Arill confirmed. "It was here where we were separated. I figured we could cover the water between here and where I found his boat, but we should keep within shouting distance of each other."

They spread out, heading west, a direction Deiji knew with assuredness, as her sense of direction was dead on and magically acute. As they swam they sang the song of the Dolphin and the tune of the Mermaid, hoping he might respond.

Arill was Mowat's dearest and oldest friend. He was a lovely Dolphin, his gray body sleek and shining in the water, though he had a few scars. Deiji loved it when he grinned, and he grinned easily, for Dolphins are cheerful creatures. Though he had been looking depressed as of late.

They were in deep ocean, and it was a hard swim before the sea floor came into focus. There was nothing on the sandy, rocky floor, save for sparse vegetation and a few fish. Another mile and Arill called out to her, "see anything?"

"No, nothing!" she shouted back. There were no signs that Mowat had been here at all, no foreign objects or disturbances in the sand.

Deiji peered at the floor, looking for shells from mussels, or parts of seaweed plants that had been torn away; anything that may suggest that a Merperson had eaten there. But there was nothing.

"Okay, Jai, we're nearly there!" Arill called out, when Deiji spotted something that made her heart skip a beat.

"Arill!" She moved her green tail fin quickly and raced to the thing. "Arill, look at this!" She snatched it up and showed it to him as he approached her, staring blankly, clearly astonished. His demeanor changed, however, and his face lit up.

"I knew it!" he cried. It was Deiji's leather arm cover, the strip she used for Polk to perch on back at Mount Odel, many years ago. "I knew it."

₪

THE BOY

Zechi was galloping fiercely along The Main Road of Odel. He saw the fork ahead on the dirt road and took it to the left, towards the mountain. The snowcapped peak of Mount Odel was clear overhead and he smiled. He had a mind to head into the Deep Forest to visit Jayna's grave, but he knew he might not have the time.

Early that morning Zechi had snuck into the castle stables and stole General Morim's best horse. He threw the saddle pad over the horse's back and rode out of the Nigh court before the sun had fully risen. He was free! He grinned when he imagined the amount of trouble he was surely in.

Zechi had spoken to Arill the day after he was forbidden to go with Deiji and Mangiat... he remembered so clearly...

בו

"There is much more at stake, Master Zechi," the Dolphin had insisted. "If they say you are to stay, you must abide by their wishes."

"But I cannot do that," Zechi countered with conviction as he treaded water. "Sounet says I have great purpose, and I am meant for this journey."

Arill looked at him sharply. "The trees told you that?"

He smiled wanly. "The trees tell me many things."

Arill was silent for a moment, deep in thought. "Then you know what it would be for me to help you?" He asked this carefully.

"I understand. I cannot pressure you to disobey our king." Zechi fell silent, wondering of another way.

"Jai has uncovered a mere tenth of her power," Arill went on without missing a beat. "One of those powers is in the ability to call forth those she wishes to speak to in a private setting where it is a guarantee there will be no interruptions. Tell me,

47

Zechi, you have read of Jai's legends and lore.
When Mowat wished to speak to her, where did he
bring her?"

"To his cave," he answered, delighted. "In the
stars."

"To his cave. And when they first met in his
cave, how did she get there?"

"You helped her... She dove into the pond on
Mount Odel." It suddenly clicked, and he smiled
broadly. "Do you think she will go back there?"

Arill sighed. "If it seems that we cannot locate
Mowat, then only Jai has the potential to establish
some sort of communication with him. If that is the
case, then we would retrace those steps. I suggest
you start there."

ℵ

Polk was flying overhead now as Zechi headed
towards the mountain. Jai's bird had decided to
come along for the journey, and he appreciated this.
He had taken Arill's advice to heart, and rode
swiftly, the countryside passing by easily. He made
it on horseback through the mountain pass and
moved to the base of the quiet volcano of the
Eastern Ranges, Mount Odel.

A shadow passed over the early morning's
sunshine, and Polk veered away, startled. His horse
spooked, and Zechi reined him in, looking to the
sky.

"Whoa," he said to his ride as he watched an
armored blue Dragon swoop down overhead and
come to a stop on the path ahead of him.

"You there, boy!" a tall, white haired man called out to him. He seemed young in age, though his face looked old. He was strong in body, and his eyes were every bit as blue as his Dragon's. He wore boots that reached up to his knees, and strange, colorless clothes. His Dragon was obviously feminine, and blue to the tips of her claws. She was sweaty beneath her metal plating, and when she stretched her body to its full extension, Zechi was stunned.

Even though Man and Mystical lived together, a Dragon was not a common sight. In fact, now that he thought of it, Zechi had not seen another Dragon since the battle on Mount Odel, other than Geo.

"Good sir!" he called out, jumping down from his horse. "May I ask your name, as well as your Dragon's?" He held the horse by the reins and took a step or two towards him. The man also dismounted and walked alongside the Dragon.

"I am Docin, the Dragon Keeper of the Dragon Islands. This is River, my Dragon and most trusted friend." The man's smile was warming, and there was something very simple and comfortable about him, so Zechi smiled.

"My friend Deiji also lives on the Dragon Islands, with her Dragon, Geo."

"Ah, yes, Geo." Docin smiled at the memory. "A very good Dragon. Missed out on some of his earlier training, but he turned out to be a very noble Dragon indeed."

"I have never really seen another," Zechi admitted, looking at River. She seemed to hold a gracefulness even Geo couldn't muster.

"Ah, yes, that is quite probable. Dragons never stray too far from the Islands anymore. They are best off living near one another and defending their Keeps."

"Then what brings you to the mainland? It is very far from your Islands."

"I am seeking a stone."

"A stone?"

"Yes," Docin continued, looking worried. "There is a special stone with a Rune encryption inscribed on it that we must find. See, there is a plant we call Dragon's Breath that grows in the ocean off the shore of the Islands. The Mermaids normally retrieve it each year, in a sort of ceremony in line with the Code. You know, live for others, help one another, that sort of thing." He rolled his eyes a bit.

"The plant is good for the Dragon's digestion, necessary even. Dragons can sometimes get it themselves, but my colony is large, and there are so many Dragons to provide for... It is difficult to gain adequate stores for them. The Merpeople have blackmailed me by withholding the plant until I find this stone for them."

"What will they do with it?" Zechi asked, curious.

"That I do not know. They were not altogether clear, but it seemed that they believed it would heal them from one thing or another."

"And how does such a stone have healing powers? Where might it be?"

"How would I know of that? My life is a simple one." Docin shrugged. "I heard a rumor I might find it in the mountains. Have you heard anything of the sort? For the sake of my Dragons, I beg you…"

"No, good Sir, but I wish you the best of luck." He turned back to his mount.

"Where are you headed this day, boy?" Docin's tone seemed suddenly sharp.

"My sister's home," Zechi said lightly without hesitating. "She is away, and I am to tend to her animals and the like." The Dragon Keeper did not seem to catch his lie, though River did stare at him very openly with her clear blue eyes, and enough for him to feel like he was caught. "I wish you the best of luck, Sir," Zechi repeated.

"My thanks, lad." They bowed and turned back to their animals and went their separate ways. Zechi rode on and around the mountain, cutting through the Odel Village, wondering at the odd man he had just met.

The Odel Village was a bustling, busy place, and it had grown considerably in the last several years, in light of Deiji's debut. It was more of a town, really.

Peasants were passing busily about, buying bread and vegetables and fish from the market stands. Elves drew water from the well, or swept the dust from their doorsteps. Children ran about the streets half naked, playing the mischievous games only children can play. Chickens squawked and women gossiped, and he could see Men working in a distant field. He saw that they all kept themselves separate in their work and play; children of Men would not join in a game with a Centaur. It was as in all the villages of Nigh.

Zechi kept his face expressionless, and tried to appear as though he belonged as he passed through the town and rode up the mountain trail.

Chapter Five
The Storm

THE KEEPER OF FIRE

"Why did he have my leather strip?" Deiji asked fervently, holding it in her fingers.

"I do not know," Arill admitted, and he swam around to her other side. He moved somewhat slowly, and for the first time she could see his age creeping up upon him. "I never saw him carry it." He turned to her, looking anxious. "Do you have any idea why Mowat needed to speak to you? Any reason at all?"

Deiji touched his face. "I know you fear for your friend, but there is nothing I can tell you. Tell me exactly what happened. Perhaps we can find the reason there."

"Whatever it was, it was very important to him. We were flying through the stars and Mowat became quite agitated, and tried to cast a healing spell. He gave no reason, just did it. And when it failed, he went into a panic. He said we had to go to the earth right then, and we fell to Toten Town, as if we could stay airborne no longer, or he couldn't land where he pleased.

"He borrowed a rowboat from a fisherman and paddled desperately across the Southern Ocean. I refused to leave his side, and I pressed for an explanation, but all that he would tell me what that he needed to see you, needed to tell you something." Their eyes met. "He said that as you grew stronger, he grew weaker. That he was nothing more than a man, now."

"That is what Zechi told Mangiat," she said gently.

Arill sighed. "Jai, you have great powers, and greater ones are coming to you. It is time for you to take on a stronger responsibility for your destiny. It is good that you have left your Island; it is time for you to take your place among the stars. Nigh is full of problems, and it is my strong belief that you hold the key. It is what Mowat expects of you, and if you follow that path, you may find out what Mowat intended, if not actually finding Mowat himself."

They were both silent for a long, long time. The water suddenly felt very cold.

"We should get back to the others," Deiji suggested, looking away. Was it good that she left her Island? Perhaps. And if she was now to take her place among the stars… The weight of such responsibility was like that of the ocean's pressure.

"Yes, but do not forget what I have said," the Dolphin said sternly. "There is much at stake here. So much."

₪

THE KING

The wind is cold here, and it blows fiercely. I find myself alone for the hour, in the company of a quiet Dragon and an arrogant cat. So I must say, this has been quite a miserable trip thus far.

Will we find Mowat? Into this thought I pour my energy, my hope, and yet the likelihood is slim… I pray things are well back in the Nigh courts, that Zechi is waiting patiently enough, and that General Morim, who has never once failed me, is governing well.

I remember a day, only a few years back, when Zechi and I were stargazing – a necessary part of his training, I thought. And he asked me, "How many worlds lay beyond, Master?" And I laughed and told him there were too many for mortals to count.

And the young boy's brow furrowed, and he said stoutly, "Jai could count them!"

I laugh now because it is true. We called upon Deiji because only she could bring the answers to all we seek. Only Jai can give solutions to these puzzles we find ourselves faced with. Beyond this, there is only one thing unknown to me: Is a king able to love freely?

Mangiat closed his journal and breathed deeply against a sharp pain in his head. He closed its leather binding and tucked it away into his bag, for he had refused to unpack any of his finer things, believing that they wouldn't be at sea much longer. Or perhaps he was wishing it.

He returned to the deck where Geo was waiting up in the shrouds, looking out to sea for any sign of his friend. It was starting to rain, so Mangiat was relieved when Deiji's head appeared between the railings. She finished the climb up the rope ladder and hopped onto the deck.

"Well?" he asked eagerly, and Geo glided down beside them. They stared at her.

"We didn't find him. But we did find something," she added, and Mangiat's heart leapt.

"What is it?"

She thrust a piece of leather into his hands and turned to the sea, her arms resting on the rail. The wind was cold, and the ocean waves were moving roughly, their tops capped with white foam.

"It used to belong to me when I lived on Mount Odel, back before... well, back before everything." She tore herself away from the railing and began to pace, obviously agitated.

Mangiat and Geo stared down at it.

"Why did he have this?" Mangiat wondered aloud. Geo sniffed at it, then looked back over his shoulder, northeast. He snorted loudly.

Mangiat looked up, but Deiji caught the cue first.

"Mount Odel," she said, her eyes still lingering over the churning waves. She turned and faced them, her expression fixed. "We have to go to Mount Odel."

₪

"No, Geo!"

The peace was broken as they set sail towards Toten Town, and Mangiat cringed. Geo's tail was caught in the ratlines, and he cut himself free, breaking the ropes.

"Puff, repair it!" Deiji commanded. Geo made a motion of apology, but she snapped at him, "forget it!" and stomped away angrily. The wind blew harder, louder. The sky had darkened and all around them was an eerie gray.

Mangiat approached Geo, who looked somewhat dejected. "Don't take it to heart, my friend. She is only a little stressed." A torrent of rain broke from the sky and they stood soaked.

"All right, *very* stressed."

The Dragon nodded a bit in understanding, then looked away. Mangiat turned towards the Captain's cabin, stumbling as he did so. He had since gained a good control of his legs and could walk easily, but he found himself unsteady once more.

"What on Earth…" He glanced up, bewildered to see Deiji was struggling too.

"What is happening?" he shouted out, for the sky had grown eerily dark, the wind was suddenly full of rain and hail, and each drop pricked like a pin.

The girl looked up to the darkened clouds, her eyes wide. "Hurricane!"

The ship was rocked around, turned mercilessly about through the angry waters. A large wave crested against the ship, tipping it dangerously onto its side. Mangiat hugged himself to a mast and saw a wall of water rolling towards him. He closed his eyes and groaned, "Not like this… Any way but this."

"Geo!" Deiji's voice was sharp and fearful. He opened his eyes to see the Dragon airborne, tossed around in the midst of the storm. He was sucked away by the angry wind, struggling to stay near them, his large, leathery wings beating fiercely.

Deiji was running, stumbling about the ship calling out orders to her cat.

"Drop the sails! Sails down! Tighten your ropes, keep the masts secure!" She climbed into the rigging.

Mangiat could feel his grip slipping. He was opening his mouth to call for help when a large wave overtook them. He found himself dragged through the gap in the rail, choking on water, two hands holding tight, his four legs wind milling. His hooves pawed against the hull and he could not think for fear. "My hands are so cold," he whispered. He could not grip.

Suddenly, Deiji swung over the edge near the bow, one hand gripping a loop at the end of a cut rope line. She ran sideways across the hull, and shouted, "take my hand!"

He gripped her forearm and she his, and she called out, "NOW, Puff Puff!" The rope tightened and drew them up and over the rail.

They collapsed in a heap, a tangled mess on the water-soaked deck, as the world continued to rock around them. Deiji grabbed his face with both hands and shouted through the clatter of the hail, "do NOT make me watch you DIE!"

And she leapt to her feet and was gone, busying herself about the ship. Lightning flashed, and he could hear thunder. The hail grew thicker, bruising his bare shoulders.

Mangiat rose to his shaking knees and made for the cabin, but another wave came, and another, and he slid across the slick deck. Just as a third one came, he lunged for the door and lost his footing on the ice.

His right hind leg gave a sickening SNAP! and he fell, rolled across the deck and into the wooden doorway.

"Mangiat!" Deiji's voice was afraid. "Mangiat! NO!" Her dark eyes were wide.

"STOP!" she screamed at the top of her lungs, and the storm stopped, as suddenly as if it had never been. The wind was quieted, the water calmed, and the clouds dissolved so the sun could shine once more. He was gasping, and she ran to his side where he lay. "Mangiat?"

They both looked at his leg and saw bone. She gasped and he groaned. "What can be done?" she asked anxiously. "Can we set it?"

"It is death." He coughed.

"What?"

"I will die. If I lay here like this for an hour or more… If I cannot stand, I will die."

Deiji's dark, starry eyes narrowed. "Not on my watch." She took his hand.

"But what could you do?" he asked, squeezing the hand of his best friend. "Deiji, I need to tell you…"

She looked at him closely, then at his wound. The bone stuck forth from the skin at an awful angle, but there was very little bleeding. She released his hand and brought all of her fingers over that spot and let them hover there, not quite touching.

He could feel a warmth, almost a glow of some sort come from her hands, and she whispered, "*Hertzel*." There was a jolt of pain and he closed his eyes to it. He felt his bones shifting, and then it was gone. All the pain, gone. He opened his eyes and looked at his leg, then wide-eyed to his friend.

"You fixed me!" He rose to his feet and tested his leg gingerly. "Not even a scar! How did you do that? That's so…" He meant to say, 'like Mowat,' but the realization came to him: *Jai is as Mowat ever was.*

"I actually learned it from a book I read, a book of dark magic."

He stared down at her.

"To completely know good, one must understand evil with a wise eye, however guardedly." She rose to her feet as well, and the two friends embraced. When they pulled apart, Deiji suddenly threw her head to the sky.

"Oh, no – Geo!" She scrambled up the mast and called for him, but the Dragon was nowhere to be found. She jumped down onto the deck. "Arill?"

They leaned over the railing and the Dolphin breached in greeting.

"Geo?" Deiji asked the sky sadly, but they knew there was no answer.

ⁿ

"Jai, we must leave for Mount Odel at once. We need to continue on our way here."

She nodded mournfully, and Mangiat placed one hand on her shoulder for comfort. "He's very smart. And he knows where we're headed next. He'll meet us there."

Deiji nodded again at his assurances, and Mangiat felt he had done well.

"Alright. Puff," she called out, "set sail for Toten Town."

Mangiat cleared his throat. "I, er, also wanted to know if we had any alternative rations for food. That substance in the pot was very..."

"Questionable?"

His eyes met hers, and they laughed. Her eyes seemed to reflect the moving waves and he found himself without a word in his throat.

Deiji smiled demurely. "Puff, down the nets."

They watched as the nets lowered themselves over the ships' side. The vessel moved along, the nets skimming the waters, and when they rose again they were full of squirming fish.

Chapter Six
The Pond

When they docked south of Toten Town the next morning, Mangiat couldn't remember loving a morning more. Once back on the land he became relaxed, composed. Even Deiji seemed to notice the changes in his mannerisms, and was peeking at him from time to time through the corner of her eyes.

"It's half a day's ride to Odel," he said cheerfully. "Shall we buy you a horse?" He envisioned her sitting nobly astride a horse as she travelled alongside him. He smiled.

"No need." Deiji grinned, fixing her sword onto its place across her back. "Puff!"

The ship suddenly shrank from where it bobbed at the docks, and turned quickly back into a fluffy cat. She looked at her master with lovely, half-closed eyes and purred until Deiji giggled.

"Come here, you."

"Tell me I'm pretty," the kitten cooed, tilting her sweet blue eyes and her puffy face. Even Mangiat felt himself under her spell, and he shook his head abruptly.

Deiji smiled. "You're very pretty. Now, let us become Centaur."

Mangiat watched, completely enthralled, as the girl and her cat joined. They melted into one: half horse, half woman, their lower body a bronze chestnut in color, in contrast to his own black body.

She still wore the top of her blue sari, and her dark hair hung loosely behind her, matching her tail. She stamped one hoof impatiently, and still he gaped. She was *lovely*. He reminded himself to breathe.

"Shall we?"

They loped up the trail together.

ןכ

GENERAL MORIM

The echo of footsteps in the Grand Entrance Hall broke General Morim from his distant thoughts. He was still mulling over the boys' disappearance. He couldn't decide which angered him more – the fact that Zechi had stolen his best horse, or that he, Morim himself, would have to account for the boys' absence upon the king's return.

He looked up to see the Elder Nia approaching the velvet throne which he had restored. He figured that Mangiat would be gone for some time, and it was only practical that he had a proper place to sit.

It was logical. He ran his calloused finger along its silken lining before giving greeting.

"Declare yourself." He held the scepter easily.

Nia stood before him, taking long draws off her slender pipe. She bowed as far as she was able, her silver hair falling over her shoulders as she leaned on her cane.

"It is I, Nia, Elder to the common people and Scribe to the king. I come bearing a message from the Nigh people."

The General glanced to the side where Gance stood as standing Scribe, his quill moving rapidly across the parchment. He cleared his throat to the Elf.

"Do not record this," he commanded. "Set aside your quill and destroy your record of Nia's arrival."

Gance complied, a strong look of satisfaction upon his narrow face.

"Both of you," Gance motioned them closer. They huddled about the throne conspiratorially.

Nia leaned in and whispered, "the Miller Bowen has rounded up quite a substantial group of Humans. He has plans to start a rebellion of the like we have not encountered."

"How many men?" Morim asked urgently.

"Six hundred. If they take up arms it may very well be the end of Mystical people's rights in this world. Men are so aggressive, and they promise they will take back this world for their own."

The General looked to Gance, whose Elvin skin was whiter than usual, though it flushed a deep red. He knew Gance detested Men for the most part, in the strong belief that Man had little to no rights to Nigh.

"It is in some people's minds to free the Elves," Nia continued.

"He is correct in his thinking," spat Gance. "Elves are not Dwarves; there is no reason they should be made to work the mines!"

"War will not make amends," Morim said slowly, "In fact, it may even bring about more suffering for your Elvin kin."

"War is the only way to ensure their freedom! Why do you think I sit so closely to the throne? I would for all of Man to die than to see my brethren beaten and dying! If war is the way, then I say we agree to it!"

"This cannot, *will* not happen to my kingdom. *The* kingdom," Morim hastily corrected himself.

"Then find another means!" The Elf was fuming.

"What do you propose I do?" Morim's tone was rather hollow. He knew what they were going to do. He stared at the stained glass window, pretending to admire the colorful patterns.

Nia's eyes glittered, and she gave a falcon's smile, though weak. "I say it is time."

They both looked at her.

"To do what, precisely?"

"We must set the king's seal to the papers." She motioned to the Elf who shuffled through his stack of parchment and produced two legal documents. They both looked at the General in earnest, who sighed with a heavy heart. He nodded. Gance handed him the papers quickly, lest he change his mind.

Nia held up a stick of colored wax over the nearest candle while Gance made ready the royal seal, the bronze stamp.

"Yes. I know it is inevitable, as King Mangiat knew," Morim said gently. "There must be a compromise for peace, even if battles are fought because of it. The citizens of Nigh will eventually settle down into their new way, even if divided." He paused. "My only worry is what Mangiat will say when he returns."

"*If* he returns," Gance drawled nastily, with a grin.

"The world aloft is quite harsh," Nia cooed. "That Centaur did not even take with him his Royal Guard. Anything can happen beyond the borders." She placed the seal into his hand herself, guiding his arm over the papers.

Morim winced at the woman's words.

"Do not be so shy, my lord," Nia said with smooth flattery. "Of all the people deserved to be king… You remain the backbone of all decisions as it were. All that has changed is the formal title."

Gance fell to one knee. "Do what is right for the kingdom. Your kingdom." He lifted his head and Morim motioned for him to stand, his brow furrowed in all confusion. The Elf leaned over him, dripping the hot wax onto each paper, and Morim set the stamp into the soft puddles.

"There we are," Gance said briskly, striding away, papers in hand. "Come, Nia, there is much to be done."

They left General Morim alone in the hall, and he watched them go, feeling terrible.

רח

THE KEEPER OF FIRE

"It's just around the pass!" Deiji yelled over her shoulder, holding herself back enough for Mangiat to keep up. She laughed at her friend, though tired. Mangiat was breathing hard, huffing and puffing as they cantered on. He was obviously pleased to be back among the brushy paths, which were, after all, nearer to his home.

"Do you think you'll be able to reach Mowat's cave from the Mountain?" he asked her, panting.

"I don't know," she admitted, "but I am sure something will come of it."

"And then what?"

"What's that?"

The Centaur grinned again as they fell into a trot. "Say we do find Mowat and all is sound. What will you do then?"

She blushed, then scolded herself silently for doing so. "Well, I hadn't really –"

Suddenly, a shadow passed overhead and both Mangiat and Deiji reared up and turned in the direction of the thing, which landed to the right of the path.

Her jaw dropped in complete surprise, for there before them was a great blue Dragon, the gaps in her armor showing her back, which was studded with Sapphires and blue Pearls. Upon it was a man, straight backed and handsome. His hair was so blonde it was almost white, his eyes blue and wide and beautiful; his skin so pale that she inwardly questioned his health. She could not tell if he were young or old. He was very handsome, but his age was inscrutable to her. He was both young and old and neither at all. He looked... *ageless*.

"Who..?" Deiji could not think for words.

"You there, Centaurs!" he called out to them, walking closer, and she blushed for the second time that day, realizing what she appeared to be. She glanced at Mangiat who indeed had seen, and he frowned.

"Please, sir, your name?" she asked politely, as was the custom. "And that of your Dragon as well."

"I am Docin, the Dragon Keeper of the Dragon Isle. This is my dearest companion, River." He nodded to the female, who shook her slender blue body vigorously. Deiji admired her planks of armor, and wondered idly if one day Geo should wear such things.

"And you?" Docin asked them as if the answer mattered little to him; it was only a gesture of courtesy.

"We are Mangiat and Jai," Mangiat interjected smoothly. "What brings you to the land of Nigh?"

"I am on a quest for a stone with a Rune encryption."

At this Deiji did not blink, but thought furiously to put her sword out of sight, and not show that she did.

"What sort of encryption?" Mangiat asked curiously, and Deiji held herself stiffly, not wanting to bring any attention to her sword.

"It has only been explained to me by rough description," Docin said, and Deiji's heart sank, for he was staring right at her, unblinking.

"River and I had set out about a week ago," the Dragon Keeper continued. "The Merpeople are withholding a certain herb we use commonly, as a means of blackmail. They will keep it from me and my Dragons until we hunt down the stone and bring it to them."

"The Mermaids," Mangiat said thoughtfully, and Deiji did not dare make eye contact with him, but they were both thinking it.

"I have been searching for it in the Mountains, but I have had no luck. I have asked a dozen villagers in this region, but mostly they're just scared of my Dragon." He chuckled a little. "Save for one, a young boy in clean peasant's clothes."

Mangiat looked up sharply at this, but the man seemed to not notice.

"I must be on my way, Centaurs. If either of you discover such a stone, keep it close to you, for I will seek you out again!" There was a great WOOSH as River spread her great wings and they rose into the sky.

"Farewell," Deiji called easily, her shoulders tense. They waited until Docin and his Dragon had disappeared before they spoke.

"Mermaids?!" they exclaimed to one another, excited. They collected themselves.

"They have Mowat. And they want the Rune," Deiji said, her face dark and sinister.

69

"They think he has it. Or at least he knows where it is." They stared at one another frowning, wondering at this new development.

"Well, at least we have a place to start."

"Let us take our time in the Odel Village before continuing on. We do not want to be followed."

Deiji nodded in agreement and glanced at her sword protectively.

ﭏ

They approached the bustling town of Mount Odel and Deiji blushed yet again. She stopped where she stood.

"What is it?" The Centaur was staring back at her quizzically.

"We should disguise ourselves so that the village folk do not see me. I do not want to be recognized."

Mangiat looked amused. "What other disguise is necessary? You are a Centaur, milady!"

Still, she wasn't convinced. "Puff, please make me look as another woman... My old Mermaid friend Elail, perhaps," she added thoughtfully.

She was pleased when her rough brown hair became a bright yellow in color, and her darkly tanned skin went bronze. She knew her nose turned up a little, and her dark eyes grew larger and became as blue as the sea itself.

"It is only until we make it up the Mountain," she explained to Mangiat who stood agape.

"Yes, I'm sure we would cause quite a scene," he said, his eyes still wide.

"Let's go. We're galloping."

70

They cantered along the main path that led through the settlement, and as soon they had entered the town square Mangiat began to shake in a fit of laughter.

"Don't," Deiji began with a scowl, but it was too late; he had seen it.

For there, in the middle of the town, sat a vegetable cart, fenced off from all else. On it stood a marble statue of a girl pointing a curved sword to the sky.

"It bears a common likeness, don't you think?" Mangiat teased, and Deiji turned even redder. "Seems you did them a good deed, eh?"

"Let's just go, okay?"

"So tell me about Elail," Mangiat called over to her as they kept an easy lope on the incline.

"She was a Mermaid. I was with her when Mowat sent me to the ocean."

"You've never spoken of her before," he said pointedly.

"There's not much to say. I helped her find her family when they had been taken by the Balla. She was a very willful creature. Fought every decision I ever made."

"Oh."

The journey up the Mountain path was quiet and quick and uncompromised, for few villagers resided there.

Deiji's old farm was silent as they reached the top of the ridge where it waited. After all she had done in years past, she had sent her parents to retire on the beaches of the coveted Trinity Islands. The warm waters of the Southern Gale would surely do them good after all that they had been through. Her Aunt Micid had disappeared shortly after Deiji's coronation. No one had heard from her since.

Thus the farm was deserted; the barn and house decrepit, the livestock long since vanished. The pond, however, seemed unchanged, and was still encrusted across the top with a thick, sour smelling algae.

"So this is where you grew up, Jai?" Mangiat was looking at all there was to see, obviously very curious. She turned her attention to the pond, embarrassed, rubbing her hands together in preparation. The farm was small, and obviously poor. There was one corral where the donkey once lived, and a chicken coup off the side of the barn that had since fallen apart.

Mangiat touched her shoulder and she jumped.

"Sorry." He looked pained.

"Oh, no, its fine."

He stepped forward abruptly and pulled her into a light embrace. "Good luck, Jai."

"Thank you," she answered, surprised. She looked down at the water, then hesitated. "I was a peasant girl."

"Pardon?"

"When I lived here... I was a simple peasant girl who was trying to escape an arranged marriage."

Mangiat frowned, but said nothing, so she continued.

"My best friend Maia was so happy for her marriage. I resented and detested her eagerness to be sold like livestock. It caused a rift in our friendship that has never truly mended, though she did send her husband's army to help us during the Battle of Odel. But it is still a truth today that we have never resumed our friendship.

"You know, all those years ago when Mowat saved me from such a fate, I was unable to see the grand scheme of things that would come from Mowat's plans and actions. He never told me about Relant's army until I actually saw them. He was protecting me. Testing me, even, as it was an unprecedented challenge that I could not prepare for."

Mangiat leaned in, listening closely, and she knew why: He had never heard her speak of her trials before. Not many had.

"These days it is easier for me to understand things as a whole…" She closed her eyes, remembering.

"I can see and… *feel*… the entire world in my head sometimes. I see that when he put me in the Deep Forest, with you," she glanced at him with a fond smile, "he meant for me to reunite the world. When he placed me in the ocean I was to calm the seas and save its people. It's funny how I did these things without knowing altogether what my objective was."

They mused on this a moment before she spoke again. "When I met the people above the clouds it was to receive council – to know I could always seek out the Sties for advice. These were things that prepared me for what I am now."

"And the Island?" Mangiat asked softly.

"What of the Island?"

"What was it for? In your training."

73

She smiled sweetly. "The Island was for me."
Deiji turned and dived into the pond, the light
greenness enveloping her, her Mermaid's tail
sprouting instantly. She sank into the pond and
swam deeper, ignoring the chill of the water. Soon
all was a murky black.

ןﬦ

THE KING

Mangiat paced around the pond's edge restlessly.
When would she surface? How she could stand
being under water... He shuddered. He admired her
bravery, though he wished he did not feel a coward
in her presence.

He glanced around the abandoned property and
the small hovel Jai once called home. The small
pasture fenced off from the barn lay vacant, and he
walked to it, resting his hand upon the rough
wooden fence a moment. He tried to imagine her as
a child, tending to her livestock with a simple
village ignorance and he laughed because he could
not see it.

A small splash of movement in the sky and he
stiffened, thinking of the man Docin and his
Dragon, but looking again he saw it was Polk.

"Polk!" he cried out, offering his arm, but the
Falcon swooped down into the barn and out of
sight.

"Polk?" He came around the corner of the fence
and approached the doorway. There was a creak and

the sound of footsteps followed by the rustling of hay, and Mangiat drew his straight bladed sword.

"Who is there? Show yourself, I am warning you to your very life if you do not!" He paused. "Present yourself to the King of Nigh, criminal!"

He stepped gingerly into the barn and saw a pile of moldy hay shifting about in the corner. "Come out or I shall stab you!" he cried in warning, brandishing his sword. He took a step towards the person, holding his stance, and he saw the corner of their brown coat peeking out from within the hay.

He plunged his hand into the pile and withdrew a squirming, sheepish boy.

"Zechi?!"

₪

Never had Mangiat been so angry.

He grabbed the boy by the tail of his coat and spat forth, "What do you do here, boy?"

Zechi seemed to be trying to hide his slight smile, which infuriated the king further. "I, er, came to join you." He brushed straw from his messy hair.

Mangiat released him, bewildered. "And how did you know we would come here?" he pressed, sheathing his sword.

"I… guessed."

"Guessed." He crossed his arms.

"Yes. I told you," he said to his mentor sternly, his eyes low but focused, "I was meant to do this."

Mangiat examined his young face for a moment, none too pleased at his attitude. "Indeed." They left

75

the barn together and headed to the pond. Mangiat looked about with curiosity.

"How did you get here? Surely you did not walk?" He eyed Zechi skeptically.

"I borrowed a horse."

"You borrowed a horse. Whose horse?"

"General Morim's." The beginnings of a smile once again began to show themselves.

"You stole General Morim's horse? Oh, he will make a cloak out of your skins, boy! How could you?"

Aside from his surprise at this, Mangiat was shocked that Zechi had managed to secure such a horse – much less ride it. The General's personal horse was known to be fiery, and quite difficult to handle. He knew the boy had talent, as he had seen him ride during his schooling, but he did not know he was as skilled as this.

Suddenly Zechi looked crestfallen. He spoke quietly. "I had to come. I was not meant to stay."

"You think you're special then, do you?"

"No... It is not like that. But Sounet insists that I am destined for something greater than that which I already am." He looked Mangiat directly in the face, his eyes strong, his back straight.

"You must obey me, Zechi!" Mangiat was exasperated.

"I have taken no such vow of obedience to my betters," Zechi said slowly, "though I do respect you greatly, as my friend and as my king. I will take your direction on this journey, but I am my own man." His expression did not falter, and Mangiat finally nodded.

76

"Do as you will. But if anything should happen to you…" His voice choked and he spat forth with passion, "you are at least to explain yourself to General Morim regarding his horse!"

Zechi grinned and they both looked to the pond. The water was murky.

נ

THE KEEPER OF FIRE

Deiji was probing the slimy bottom of the pond, searching earnestly for the tunnel that would lead her to Mowat's cave, or even the little pocket of air where she had first met Arill. But there was nothing.

"Mowat!" she called out in frustration, anger burning in her breast. She placed her fingers against the rocky sides, wondering…

There was nothing here. She gave up and swam to the surface, her wide eyes settling on two figures standing at the pond's edge, waiting.

"Zechi?"

Chapter Seven
The Pirates

"*A*re you sure?"

Deiji glanced over as Zechi slapped the rear of General Morim's horse. They stood on the shore south of Toten Town and watched as it galloped away. Mangiat placed his hand on Zechi's shoulder, who said with a tone of assuredness, "yes, I am sure. He will find his own way back to the Nigh stables."

Deiji, however, was distracted. Geo had not met them on the mountaintop as they had guessed he would. She hoped he was all right. "Puff, the ship!" she called out carelessly, and she plunged into the restless, churning water where Arill was waiting, leaving Mangiat and Zechi to watch the ship take form. She swam up to him, kicking her green Mermaid's tail quickly.

"What has happened?" Arill asked her desperately.

78

"Zechi has come to join us."

"Has he now?" The Dolphin's face broke into a smile so cheerful that Deiji now knew exactly how Zechi had come about.

"The cave is not to be found," she announced. "It must be in another realm. I feel it is a place I can almost touch, but cannot quite find the words for."

Arill smiled as only Dolphins can smile, and answered smoothly, "then that is probably the case, my friend." He looked at her eagerly. "Jai, the whole world and the worlds of all are open to you now. You can float above the clouds with the Sties at will. You can view the world as a whole if only you ask it. I have seen Mowat do all these things…" His voice faded, and she found him to be truly sad.

He tried to smile again. "Look inside yourself, Jai. Mowat's cave exists in your mind. Will it to be so. It is your cave, now," he added.

Deiji shut her eyes and focused with all her yearning of going to that place… The cave with the open space of endless black spread out in the distance behind her. Where a simple word, thought or emotion would reflect upon the cave's lighting. It was a place of infinite respite, where no time actually passed. She frowned in concentration.

She opened her eyes to peek and gasped. Here she was! The cave was wide and open, the dome of space bright and lonely and inviting. Mowat's scales sat nearby looking oddly off-kilter.

The stars stretched on into the infinity of space. It was more beautiful than she remembered, from when Mowat had brought her here. But it was hers, now.

Deiji saw a star in the vast distance, shining a little brighter than the rest, and she wondered… Suddenly, it came to her! It drew itself between her hands and grew smaller – a bright, burning sun in a streak of color – as a string of planets around it grew bigger. A green earth rotated on its axis and she could see a blur of land and sea, cities and people and roads. It spun closer to her, and she could see things of the like she could not imagine, nor understand.

Startled, she made as though to push it away, and it zipped back to take its place among the stars once again, leaving her breathing quite heavily in shock.

She suddenly understood what she was.

Deiji looked away and found herself staring at the unbalanced scales once more. A brown piece of tattered parchment she had not noticed before caught her eye. She stretched forth one hand and it flew quickly into her grasp. She read the inscription twice over:

There is an Island of jewels
Far beyond the Western Sea.
There you will find the answer;
There you will find me.
The Rune of life is in danger, and in this danger it stays.
Keep it close to your heart, Jai, forever and always.
The Merpeople seek protection; they see it in the Rune.
There is another way to do this. You will have to choose.

*Beware of nomadic rogues who wander 'cross
the sea;
They may rob you of your riches; keep your
treasure close to thee.*

She paused, furrowed her brow, and read it
again. It was from Mowat, assuredly. She tucked it
inside an inner pocket and willed herself out of her
cave and back to the shore where her friends waited
to cast off.

She was still in the water, and Arill's eyes met
hers, beaming.

"You found it!" he exulted, without question.

"Yes," she said grimly, "listen to this." She read
the riddle to him, and the Dolphin's eyes widened.

"Who are these 'nomadic rogues?'" she asked
him. "Do you know what exists west of Treehorn
Island?"

"No. No, I have never been there. Not many
have." He looked at her, inquiring.

"See, the maps of the Known World that I knew
from the Blacksmith's shed hardly showed that
which lay inside the Deep Forest," she explained.
"The rest of the map was blank. When I retired to
the Island for all those years, I found maps inside
the Dragon's Keep. Completed maps. I've studied
them, again and again over the years, and I've
memorized every inch of this world."

"Then what lies beyond the Western Sea? What
is there that we must avoid?"

"Well," she began carefully, "on the opposite
shore of the west where the Deep Forest ends exists
the Lost Marshes. It's simple marshland, really. A

flooded bit that sits on the shoreline. But off the shore, north of there?" she hesitated.

"What is it? What is there?"

"The Pirate's Islands."

₪

THE KING

Mangiat could tell that Deiji was bothered by something when she clambered out of the water and met them on the shore. Her face was sullen, her mind elsewhere.

He looked at the ship, which sat this time, not out on the edge of the bay, but right off the shore, almost close enough in the shallow waters that he could touch it. He stared upwards. Geo was gone. So how was he to get onto the ship? Not that he really wanted to…

He looked helplessly at Deiji, who called out impatiently, "Puff, give us a ramp!"

A wooden ramp extracted from the ship and set down with a clunk upon the beach, and he followed Zechi onto the deck. The boy flinched before he walked onto the deck, and Mangiat knew this seemed unnatural to Zechi as well. He looked at Deiji who had followed.

"Where are we headed?" He stood steady while Deiji wandered about the ship, his heart quickening with curiosity. She was calling to Puff Puff to tighten this line or that, obviously irritated about something.

"The Western Sea." She fumbled through her pockets and withdrew the poem and handed it to him, turning her attention back to the ship.

He read it over, then again, his concern written on his face, then he handed it to Zechi. The ship gave a great lurch as the sails caught air, and they rushed away from the shore. Deiji was staring south, and giving Puff instructions.

"We will sail around the peninsula by the Lost Marshes. Hug the shoreline to cut our time short," Deiji announced over the roaring wind, and Zechi nodded in agreement. "It should only be a day north or so before we pass by the Pirate's Islands."

Mangiat watched her, wondering what else he could do to help. He moved towards her, but she turned away from him, resting her forearms on the railing, her eyes searching the skies and the open horizon.

₪

When he woke the next morning, Zechi was still asleep on the couch nearby, but Deiji's bed was empty. He smoothed his black hair and made his way onto the deck.

He saw her instantly, still leaning against the rail in her thin sari, despite the morning's fog. He could barely see the shore of the Lost Marshes in the distance.

"Deiji!" he said sternly, quickening his pace. He put his hands to her arms and pulled her into a sort of hug, rubbing warmth into her icy skin. "Look at you! Have you been out here all night?"

"Since daybreak," she admitted.

"What on Earth are you doing, my friend? Puff, a blanket! Now!"

The cat gave no response and Deiji waved one hand permissively. "Yes, yes, do as Mangiat says, Puff."

A neatly folded woolen blanket appeared on the deck. He snatched it up and wrapped it tightly around her shoulders, but did not release her from his embrace.

"Now what were you doing?" he asked gently. A few stars were still visible from the night, and he looked up to them for meaning, out of habit.

"I was looking for Geo. I really thought he would have shown up by now."

"Geo is very intelligent, and he can certainly take care of himself. He will be here when he finds us."

"I know. I just wish I hadn't yelled at him like I did. Do you think he left me?"

He touched her cheek. "Not at all. He forgives you."

Deiji smiled. "I know you are correct in your words."

Mangiat flinched at an inner pain, and the girl looked concerned.

"How do you fare these days, my friend?"

"I am fine, fine. I am sure we could both use something hot to drink. Is there tea in the galley?" he asked doubtfully.

"Yes."

He laughed, forcing some cheer into his voice. "Then perhaps you can help me find it!"

Mangiat ushered them along into the little room and had Deiji sit upon a stool while he busied himself with the kettle. She pointed at a small patterned tin that sat beside the pans.

"What treasure do you possess that Mowat insists you keep so guarded?" He spoke softly, for the wind only whistled through the slats of this sheltered place, and the ship creaked and groaned to its sway. He slid a ceramic mug to her, its poor black stuff clouding the boiling water. She breathed of the steam and warmed her hands to it before answering.

"The Rune of Life."

He stared. "You actually have the Rune in your possession?"

"I keep it on my sword."

She unfastened the sword from her waist and laid it upon the rough wooden table. They both leaned over and examined it. It was a beautiful thing, made of folded steel, and there was a Dragon etching on the blade. A pair of Dragons wrapped themselves around the handle, and in the center between them lay the Rune of Life.

The stone was breathtaking, a deep blue-green that seemed to glow of its own accord, as if nothing in nature could have produced such a color. Around its edges sat a curious Rune encryption.

"What does it say?"

"I have only been able to translate a mere part of it. It reads: *'Only in the darkness...'*"

"And the Merpeople want it," Mangiat said, pulling the paper from his leather waistband and reading it over again. "I believe it means we are to go to Treehorn Island. The Island of Jewels, as it is known in the Nigh court. And I think he means well when he says to protect the Rune," he added sternly. He passed the paper to Deiji who read it with great concentration.

"Keep it close to your heart..."

The Centaur looked to his companion who seemed lost in her thoughts for an eternity. After a moment's time of hemming and hawing, she muttered, *"Sieolga,"* and the knot on the back of her necklace undid itself and she caught the pendant in her fingers.

She lifted the hem of her sari to reveal a slender knife fastened to her ankle, and Mangiat nearly laughed. He watched her pry the Rune of Life from the sword, and then follow suit with the large black stone on her necklace. She switched them, pushing the Rune into her medallion with a snap! and the black stone onto her sword.

She tied the Rune of Life around her neck, and placed the sword, which was quite ordinary now, at her side. She gave him a satisfied smile and he felt odd for a moment.

"No one will ever know of this but us." She placed her warmed hand over his across the table, and they heard the sound of rapidly approaching footsteps.

"Ah, Zechi must be awake," Mangiat said, withdrawing his hand and busying himself with the dishes.

Indeed, Zechi burst through the door, but before they could call out in greeting, he shouted forth, "A ship!"

"What?" the Centaur and the girl exclaimed together.

"There's a ship," he said steadily. "I think they might be Pirates!"

נּ

THE BOY

"Pirates?"

Zechi stood beside them as they gazed over the railing at the ship that was swiftly approaching them. It had three tall masts, was slightly larger than their own ship, and it carried a tattered black flag with a crudely painted skull on it. It certainly did inspire fear.

He had never seen anything like it, and he glanced at Mangiat, who shrugged. They looked at Deiji.

"I've seen them in books," she whispered, staring at the gray sea. She held herself as though in a trance as the ship made its way quickly and deliberately in their direction. "Oh, no." She suddenly seemed to come to, and shouted, "Puff! Slacken the sails, just a little! Move us as fast as you can, northwest! *Azioni!*" The ship gave a great lurch as it was rushed forward, and she continued to shout her commands.

"Send up a white flag! A white flag! But prep the cannons!"

Mangiat turned to him. "Get below."

"I cannot do that, my king," Zechi said smoothly, and he bowed to show his respect.

87

His teacher grabbed him by the shoulders, a startling movement. They glanced at the oncoming ship. Though they moved quickly, it was still gaining.

"Do as I say!" Mangiat begged him. Zechi pulled away but did not obey. He held himself steadfast, ignoring his pleas.

They tore through the waters violently, sending a strong wake in all directions. Zechi saw Arill riding one of the waves, trying desperately to keep up.

Mangiat moved as though to wrestle the boy to the deck, when there was a CRAAAACK as the other ship rammed into them, and they all fell in a flurry of hooves and limbs. He could hear shouts and thud after thud as men swung from ropes off their ship and onto *The Princess Puff Puff*.

"Take their sails down!" a gruff voice called out, and half a dozen men spread across the ship's deck. "Take the crew!"

Zechi fumbled within his leather pouch, grabbed a Sapphire and thrust it under his tongue, tucking the rest away out of sight. He looked from where he lay upon the deck. The voice belonged to a man, a tall and angry man. He was the only one out of the score wearing boots, though they were frayed and shiny from where the leather had worn.

He seemed to hold himself with some sort of dignity, and with his lip curled under his black mustache, as though he had once been a learned man, but had fallen into this distasteful trade. Zechi quickly noted the sharp sword girded to his belt. His was the only one that possessed a sheath.

This man barely glanced at his captives as he shouted orders to his men. He spoke with such an authority that Zechi took it that this man was Captain. And it was this man who ordered them to be taken.

Another wave of crew set upon them, and before they could protest, Mangiat, Deiji and Zechi found themselves bound to the main mast after a brief struggle. They were staring into the face of a very fierce man, red haired and unshaven. He leered at them, revealing three bronze teeth amidst rotted gaps.

His face was brown and reddened from the sun. His rough, uncombed hair was held back by a scrap of a red kerchief. He looked positively filthy, but Zechi did not draw himself back as the man gave a false start in idle threat.

"What 'ave we 'ere, men?" this second man growled. There were guffaws of laughter as the man began sizing them up. "A boy an' a girl," he said passively with a lisp. "An' a Centaur. Don't see much of *your* kind on th' ships." He eyed Mangiat and spat upon the deck.

"That is enough, Ruan," the man he perceived to be Captain said calmly. Ruan pulled back his lips to reveal his broken teeth and blackened tongue once more before merging back into the crowd of Pirates.

"Where did you get that coat?" Mangiat's voice rang sharply, and all looked at him in surprise.

The Captain frowned. "What is it to you, Centaur?"

"It is the jacket of a sailing Merchant out of Nigh," he said smoothly, and indeed, Zechi recognized its deep color and its big brass buttons. It looked quite new.

The Captain offered a simple smile. "We overtook just such a Merchant's ship in this very sea a short time ago. We took many things from their crew. It is a good thing to see that the people of Nigh are making passage through these waters now, for we have been in need of supplies."

"What did you do with the ship?"

"I added it to my fleet. Have you any more useless questions? For you will not live to tell the answers to your betters."

Mangiat said no more, his expression still and unreadable.

"Sir! The sails!"

"What is it?" he barked. Two men came sprinting across the deck, their faces twisted in confusion.

"Captain, the lines. They wun be drawn in, sir."

"Then cut them!" he snapped. "They will be replaced."

"Aye, aye!" The men hurried away, and the Captain turned to his prisoners. His simpering smile faded.

"You there!" he called out sharply, and Zechi's heart sank when he realized the Captain was looking at Deiji. He strained against his bonds to see. Deiji had already freed herself.

"Ruan! Tie her up, and properly!" He was clearly irritated. Zechi found himself surprised in the man's speech. He spoke as one learned, not as one simple in mind as his crew.

Ruan and two others wrapped a length of rope around her wrists and stood back, satisfied.

Zechi heard her mutter, *"Sieolga!"* He twisted his neck until it burned, and saw her mutter it a second time. Her amulet untied itself, fell into the nape of her Sari and disappeared.

He continued to struggle against his own bonds when the Pirates saw Deiji was free again. The Captain called out, his face red with his irritation, "well, and what?"

The few nearest to her gathered round to tie her, and saw her freed yet again. The Captain straightened his collar and closed in on her like a hungry shark. "And what exactly do we have here," he drawled.

"A freak, that's what," a voice called out from behind him, and a stout, robust woman made her way to the front of the crowd. "Hello, Deiji," the woman said coldly, and he heard Deiji gasp. His eyes shot from his friend to this pig-faced woman with confusion. Who was she?

"Hello, Aunt Micid." Deiji's voice was equally cold, and she seemed too surprised to untie herself again. The wind blew fierce all of a sudden, the gusts frozen and powerful. He could feel the anger and excitement build up from inside her. "So this is where you've been."

Zechi knew little of Deiji's life with her aunt, but he could see plainly that it wasn't a pleasant one. This woman had messy dark hair, yanked back to the nape of her neck. It hung freely there, knotted into clumps, and it looked as though she had never once brushed it. A piece of rope was tied taut

91

around her great middle, holding the loose slacks she wore. Her clothes seemed to be made out of canvas, and they were filthy.

"Don't even start with me, child," Micid snapped. "After that stunt you pulled in the village, and the war? Where else could I go, but to join castoffs of my own breed? You took care of your parents well enough, but left the farm to waste. Was I to toil away, alone in such sufferings with no servant to help?" She glared at her niece.

"How did you find these men?" Deiji actually sounded curious, and Zechi wondered too.

"Well, you left no appeal for me in the Nigh court, and there was no place left for me in this World. I stowed away on a trade ship and found myself on Treehorn Island. I was caught and put to slavery in the mines, where I discovered I possess a love of jewels." She laughed richly, holding her great belly.

"I stole a row boat and made my way to what is called the Lost Marshes, and I found myself in the company of these fine men." She motioned to the sailors beside her. "Instead of slitting my throat like the others, they took me on. I must say, I've adapted to their life quite easily." Micid laughed loudly, her girth jiggling eagerly, so that Zechi felt himself sick. It was only then that he noticed the strings and strings of pearls around her neck, and each fat finger held a ring of a different jeweled stone. He was suddenly uneasy.

"Captain Farlane," the woman said flirtatiously, "May I?" She batted her sparse eyelashes at the Captain, who shrugged.

"Search them, every one of them!" Micid's voice became angry and larger than any man's, and just as gruff. "Every bit of treasure you find is to be shown to me first!"

It was a quick search. Mangiat had nothing, for he had left his crown back at the castle, and all of his knives and possessions were still below deck. Deiji's sword was taken, and the Captain held his hand for it right away, for it was such a show of craftsmanship, and a coveted piece for a Captain to have. Her pendant was not discovered.

Zechi, however, knew that his little leather bag of Sapphires lay hot in his breast. Sure enough, Ruan pulled them from his inner pocket and broke the string from Zechi's neck, dousing him with his horrid breath before presenting the jewels to Micid.

"Ah!" she cried, delighted, "a true treasure!" The woman sighed in some satisfaction, and Zechi felt an unholy anger well up inside him.

"No!" he called out, and the Pirates laughed. "No, you cannot have those. Anything else you can have, but not those!"

Deiji slipped from her bonds once more and stood up. Her voice was loud and clear, and even her enemies paused to give their ear. "Let the boy have his treasure. I will take you to a Dragon's Keep I know of, which contains piles and vast piles of treasure more glorious than his, and you may have it all."

Captain Farlane gave her a very doubtful look, and although Zechi's eyes stung with the edge of tears he could still see a faint scar where the man's lip had once been torn.

"It is a curious thing, lass, that you would try to lure us into the cave of a Dragon."

"Hear hear!" the men called out and whistled.

"No, no," she insisted, and Zechi's heart was warmed. Here was his dearest hero, the fabled peasant girl, defending him! "The Dragon is long since gone. It is where I have lived these last five years. I know the island very well. There is even a treasure chest —"

A murmur ran through the gathered men and the Captain held up one hand to silence them. "I have heard enough. Shall we go to her Island, men?"

"Aye, aye!"

And another called out, "this ship will none be moved, sir!"

"Lock them in the brig!" Captain Farlane snapped. "We set sail for the Dragon Islands! Leave this troublesome ship be, men, and cast her anchor! We will return to her shortly." He turned to Deiji. "You will come to my cabin and show me the course to your Island."

Zechi found himself dragged, carried roughly alongside Deiji across a ramp onto the Pirate's own ship, *The Lantern*, and down into their ship's hull. Mangiat was too awkward with his four legs, and he could not be led below, but was led across the ramp, and tied to their mast.

"Puff!" he heard Deiji whisper as they left the ship, "find Geo and bring him to our Island! Tell him it is time to defend his Keep."

ןּ

Zechi was alone in the dark for quite some time before Deiji joined him in the brig. She untied his bonds immediately and sat beside him on a broken crate. The floor of the hull was very wet, and they were cast into complete darkness without a second thought by their captors. It was frigid and musty in here, and he rested his head upon the cold bars.

"What do I do if they question me?" he asked. He could plainly imagine what they did to those they found no value in.

She placed a comforting hand on his shoulder. "Just go along with whatever they say to do. I will be there to protect you."

He braced himself against the chill. They were stuck for the time, heading in the wrong direction, each minute taking them farther and farther from Mowat.

It was completely dark and he wished he could see Deiji's face. He knew she could make light if she wished it, but she seemed to be of dampened spirits. He wondered why she did not save them. *"Were things always this bad?"* he wondered in the quiet of his mind. He supposed they were.

ꑐ

SIX YEARS AGO…

"Let's go, Zechi!" Adene's voice rang out in its high pitch as she ushered him out of the rickety schoolhouse and into the sun. It was a nice afternoon in Toten Town, and he knew she wanted to see the horses.

She turned back to him. The sun was bright on her yellow hair, and she flashed him a baby-sweet smile. Her cloak was as pink as summer strawberries, and it suited her, for she was two years younger than he.

School had been pleasant that day. It was warm enough that they did not have to light the stove and take turns standing at it for its heat. Besides, the teacher hadn't singled him out once. He did well enough in school, for he had an eager mind, though he was shy, and felt too shy for such learning among the boisterous village children. But it was better than being at home, or among the scrupulous villagers.

Toten Town's inhabitants were descendants of a proud nomad culture – the first band of Man to travel outside the Nigh villages and settle on the river shore. He was of the third generation to settle here.

Zechi was confident and able in one area only: horsemanship. How fortunate was he, that his mother's position in the town was horse trainer? He was the secret envy of every child in the village, though this did little to bring him friends. It was not generally smiled upon by the village Elders, but his mother was insistent that Zechi assist her in the breaking and training of any horses that came through their stables. It was because of her zealousness that Zechi spent most of his childhood on the strong back of Baal, the village work horse.

Zechi and Adene passed through the village easily, for all were pleasant people. Toten Town experienced little hardship, save for the earthquake they must endure once a year. It was nothing to be questioned, as it was inevitable, but there were still those who complained heartily at its inconvenience. Aside from this, life was peaceful here.

Zechi walked briskly, trying to match Adene's pace as they hurried to the corral. "Hold on, Adene!" he called as he finally broke into a run to keep up. She was a lot of responsibility, and he felt compelled to keep her under his eye.

Adene did not turn to face him as she shouted forth, "But she said the horses would be there today!" She was skipping down the path into town, and Zechi had to smile. She was always cheery, and it was enough to lighten anyone's spirits.

A mare and a weaned foal had been captured from the wild herds that wandered between Mount Odel and Toten Town. They were said to be in the village corral this very day. The Nigh court bred most of these horses among the court's own stables. Once reared and given three years of training and handling, they were released to the herds again, to live wild until reclaimed. Toten Town had paid for the breeding and rearing of a mare several years ago, and that mare had reared a foal in the wild. They were to be brought here today, a double treasure from their one payment.

Such horses were exceedingly valuable to the villagers' lives; horses they could yoke to the mill to grind flour, or to the plow to turn the fields. Sure enough, as they rounded the path they could see two new horses in the pasture. Half a dozen villagers stood nearby, one of which was Zechi's mother, Miri.

97

Miri was a pleasant woman, with easy eyes and a simple smile. She was always neat in her appearance and never seemed harried or rushed. However, she was not afraid to take to hard labor or get her hands dirty, and Zechi liked this about his mother.

The two horses were frantic, and Zechi joined Adene where she leaned against the fence. The young one was a sleek chestnut with white markings, but the larger one was blacker than coal, with wide, wild eyes.

"Gosh," he whispered in remarks to the horses' beauty and fierceness. They were powerful work animals, and the people of Toten Town would be ecstatic when they saw these two. The village had at this time but one horse, the elderly gray thing named Baal, who was frail and no longer fit for the labors the villagers required of it. He would be released back into the wild herds of Nigh to live out his final days. This was good fortune.

He watched Miri approach the black one with seeming fearlessness, and he felt a swell of pride for his mother. She lifted the rope slowly, aiming to throw it around the horse's neck. His heart pounded. He had seen her do this before; there was much risk involved. She could be dragged, or she might drop the rope, and the horse might stumble and injure itself over it. And she would be responsible if one of these valuable animals were hurt. He held his breath.

"Easy, easy," Miri said soothingly as she approached the horse. She extended one hand

*slowly and the mare breathed heavily, and as if in a
trance as the hand met its nose.*

*It reared up without warning, knocking Miri
back into the grass. The mare ran to the far corner
beside her foal.*

*"Give her some time," Miri called to her crew as
she stood and dusted herself off. "Let's leave them
be so they can explore their new home."*

*They left through the gate, and Miri came last,
latching it securely behind her. She saw Adene and
Zechi and smiled.*

*"Hey, you two!" She began winding up the rope.
"How was school?"*

*"Fine," Zechi mumbled, and Adene cried out
with spirit, "Teacher punished me today!"*

"And why was that?"

*"The class was talking about the horses, and
Teacher asked me to say something about them. I
told her that some horses have wings," the little girl
painfully admitted, and looked as though she hoped
Miri would laugh. Zechi was not surprised when
she grew stern instead.*

*"You know that these are only stories, right?"
Miri's voice was loud, and as clear as water under
ice. She cupped the girl by the chin and held her
face steady so that the girl must meet her eyes.*

"Yes, ma'am."

*Miri released her hold forcefully and the girl fell
silent. She began to pluck daisies from the green
grass as they walked along, humming softly to
herself. Miri turned to him and he braced himself.*

"Zechi, your father craves a word with you."

His shoulders slumped and he found himself staring at the ground, wanting to be somewhere else, anywhere else.

While his mother worked with the village livestock, his father Harlkene was a butcher, fixated on the notion that he must find and secure a place in a proper trade for Zechi; a life's work to earn his bread.

Zechi had long since dreaded any sort of talk, and he certainly did not want to be pulled out of the school as all young boys were when they took to a trade. He was not eager to grasp at the offer his father sought high and low for. It seemed to him a matter of his own choosing, and he would choose his life when he had decided what it was to be. But his father differed in this opinion.

"A man must have a trade," Harlkene insisted as he cast about for such a place for his son, counting the money he had saved that one must pay for apprenticeship training. And it was such a conversation Zechi treaded to on this day, quite unwilling.

Their house was small and simple; two rooms, the walls earthen, the roof thatched with mud and straw. It sat in one corner of the corral, and Zechi always thought it pleasant to wake to the sight of horses grazing in the morning beside the tree.

His father sat upon a chair of bound sticks in the corner that served as a kitchen. His face was deeply inset with wrinkles, as if he had frowned always, and the lines stayed there even when he softened his expression. He was neatly shaven as always, and his broad shoulders and thick arms showed through the taut fabric of his rolled up sleeves.

"Zechi!" he said cheerfully, looking up from the wooden piece on which he whittled the shape of a horse.

"What are you working on, Father?" He turned the subject away, as if he could keep the conversation from happening.

"It's a gift for Adene, for the village ceremony tomorrow. We have been waiting quite some time for these horses. There is to be a holiday!" There was too much cheer in his voice and Zechi did not answer, remaining mute and shy before him.

Harlkene stood and brushed shavings off his lap. Zechi could see his bloodstained butcher's apron draped over the chair behind him and he looked away. He did not like blood, and was too squeamish for such things.

"The day becomes better!" Harlkene continued with enthusiasm. He placed one proud hand on Zechi's shoulder. "I have found a good trade for you, m'boy! I spoke to the Blacksmith, and he will accept you as apprentice!"

There were no words to be had at this, and Zechi's chin nearly wobbled for tears.

"Well, what do you say, boy?" His father was smiling, though his voice held tones of warning.

"Thank you, my father," Zechi said meekly.

"Rest well tonight," Harlkene exclaimed as Miri entered the house, "for tomorrow you leave that school of yours to become a Blacksmith!"

ℸ

Zechi bowed his head and muttered excuses to be away, his face ashen and ashamed because he did not want to obey his father. But in the end he must. And so his heart was divided.

He walked into the corral, his mood lifting a little to see the new wild horses in all their fierceness. But wait... He frowned and peered closer.

In the far corner of the pasture he could see the chestnut mare alongside the black one, prancing about in their small pen, and moving as though spooked... And between them, standing still and scared, stood Adene.

"Adene!" he cried, and he ran as fast as he could, scraping his knee as he scrambled between the wooden rails. The black horse reared up to her full height, and Adene's blue eyes were wide with fear... Zechi dove and grabbed her around the waist. She cried out as they rolled through the mud and into the fence.

The horses began bolting from one corner to another, their hooves thundering across the ground, their motions wild, tossing their heads and squealing.

"Over the fence, Adene!" He boosted her up before she was ready and she fell over the side. Zechi scrambled over after her, and the black mare bolted straight at the fence and did not stop.

CRAAAACK! The horse broke through the fence and let out a neigh of triumph as she and her foal galloped off through the village.

Zechi helped Adene to her feet. "Are you alright?"

"Yes," she whispered. Her already pale skin was unusually white.

They could hear the cries of the villagers as the horses tore through the crowds and their market stands. Miri and Harlkene came dashing out of the house, pausing only to cast brief, horrified looks at them before chasing after the mares.

The horses escaped.

That evening, the honored Elder Nia made an appearance at Zechi's doorstep with a small band of supporting Elders. After a heated exchange of words between them and Zechi's parents, they led Zechi and Adene before the entire village, into the middle of the town square.

"This boy," Nia announced to the gathering crowd, shrugging her purple shawl across her shoulders, "and this girl, eight and six years old in their ages, have lost us the two prized horses we have long awaited from the wild herds."

There was a murmur from the crowd as they accepted this new truth.

"As children, we are more lenient to such faults. However, due to the gravity of the offence, punishment will ensue. There will be a great fine that we cannot pay for the men of Nigh to recapture these horses! We shall be chastised for losing our lot."

The crowd huffed in their upset, whispering amongst each other.

Nia's voice was as cold as her gray eyes.

"Therefore I say, give him three lashes, and spare

the girl!" The people cheered, and she went on. "In light of these circumstances, let the parents pick the punishment for the younger of the two."

Zechi held his head low. There would be no good outcome to this.

A man stepped to the front of the crowd clutching his blackened hat, and he cleared his throat. Zechi's head snapped up. It was the Blacksmith.

"Speak your piece, Blacksmith," Nia spat, as if afraid he would say something in the boy's defense. As the village Head and dealer of all affairs, Nia knew of the upcoming apprenticeship.

"I... I will take no such troublemaker into my shops," he said haltingly, and Zechi's heart sank even lower, for he knew his father glowered at him. Sure enough, Zechi braved a glance, and Harlkene tossed the little carved horse at his feet.

Zechi winced, and his father's voice came loud, "you have shamed me! You have thrown your future to the dogs! You are worth nothing as a son! Beat him, I say! Give him his three lashes and more, which are his due!"

He began to sob and could not bear it any longer. He snatched up the carving and fled, the Village Elder's voice following him on the wind, plaguing him.

"A shame! A shame on this boy and his sister."

₪

He ran north, alongside the Longest River, until he could run no more. The air in his lungs was ragged, and his blood ran hot. He fell to a walk, his sweat now cold on his body, and he wondered at the thickness of the trees on either side of him. He had never ventured here before, and he wondered, doubtfully, if many had.

The sun was setting now and he must go back. He felt a coward for leaving Adene to suffer punishment alone. Being an older brother certainly had its moments.

He stared at the rushing river a while as he walked, the river that divided the Known and Unknown worlds from each other. A tree had fallen across the water, an easy bridge between shores. It seemed like such a simple division, and he wondered why it was so forbidden to cross it.

Toten Town was the closest settlement to the Unknown part of the world, and it was quite secluded as well, the nearest village being that of Mount Odel, which lay some miles north.

Zechi walked across the fallen tree without hesitation, a zealous rebelliousness burning in his breast.

"Oh!" he cried. He slipped on a spot where the bark was rubbed off, and he fell into the River with a splash. It was deeper than it seemed, a dark hole beneath the log. It was muddy and murky, but he could swim, and he hauled himself out onto the other side.

Considering the place, he bent a long branch jutting from the log until it snapped; a reminder that it was easy to slip there. Once across he felt sure that heaven would smite him, but there was nothing here but more trees. A shiny, quick movement caught his eye. "What kind of insect is that?" he wondered aloud.

It was tiny, no bigger than the nail on his pinky finger, but two large wings fluttered at its sides. It was glowing, as if it had a white aura, and it sparkled prettily. Zechi gasped as he saw it bore beautiful, minute features.

"Is that a Fairy?" he cried, and the thing zipped away and was gone. This was incredible - it was significant. A fairy, from the stories of old. If indeed such things existed then there was more to this land than he ever thought possible.

He wandered alone again until the world was black, and he lay under some bushes shivering against the night's damp coldness. As he huddled there, he wondered if he could ever face what awaited him back home.

נ

The birds were chirping in the early morning's light when Zechi awoke and rose groggily to his feet.

"Oh!" a little voice cried, and Zechi looked around.

A small brown rabbit was staring at him, had been watching him as he slept. Its nose was twitching. Zechi frowned at it.

"Did you just..?" But before he could finish his question, the rabbit hopped off into the bushes.

He treaded farther and farther into the Deep Forest, wondering at the Unknown world, which seemed not so different than his own, though wholly new to him. It was something about the animals and the trees. He knew not where he was headed as he wandered; only he meant to delay his homecoming.

A spot of white caught his eye, and figure rushing up the slope. A wolf! It was pure white, and it paused at the crest of the hill and sat there, in his path.

They stared at one another. The wolf's eyes were an icy blue, and it had a large mane that fit close to its body. The animal stared at him for a while longer, then turned and walked into the forest. He was compelled to follow, for he was certain the wolf would not harm him.

He had just entered a small, sunny clearing when he heard a voice.

"Child, are you lost?"

The voice was soft and pleasant, so he did not jump at its suddenness. The wolf had disappeared. He looked about for the source of the voice and found himself staring, agape.

It was a woman, and she appeared to be growing from a tree. Her waist melted into the tree trunk and her features seemed carefully carved. Her hair was a long, green sheet of ivy, and she wore a moss tunic over her delicate wooden figure.

"Who... what are you?" he asked, aghast. Zechi could not tear his eyes away from this regal creature, and was stunned when her oaken chest moved in and out – she was breathing!

"I am the Queen of the Forest." Her answer was simple, her expression eternally sad.

Zechi sank to one knee in reverence.

She asked him again, "what do you do this far onto the opposite shore? Are you lost?"

"No, milady. I can find my way home from here. I... I ran away."

"And why do you run, my child?"

And so Zechi poured out his heart to this creature in his bitterness. How he had disappointed his father's efforts, how his sister had caused such trouble and he was to suffer for it, for children's voices mean nothing among men. He sat there and sobbed awhile, not understanding how this odd tree of a woman existed, or why she cared.

"What is your name?" she asked finally.

"Zechi." He wiped his wetted nose along his sleeve. "What's yours?"

"Jayna."

"I am glad we met, Jayna."

She smiled, a beautiful smile that carried with it the sadness of centuries. "Cease to cry so, my young friend. You have a destiny greater than that which your father or your clan had planned for you. Return to your home, and return with your head held high. You will face your punishment and obey your elders until you come of age. And one day, when you are old enough to seek your own mind, you will discover my meaning."

"I have... a destiny?"

She smiled. "Go."

He rose to his feet and nodded, already brave. He turned to walk back to the river.

"Zechi!"

He turned back. "Yes, milady?"

"Tell no one we have met or spoken. Not all men are as wise in their thoughts as yourself."

He agreed to keep a silence and made his way back to the homestead by nightfall. He discovered that because he had run, his sentence had been moved up from three lashes to five, and he accepted this without comment or complaint.

Miri and Harlkene did not punish Adene, save for a scolding, but neither would look Zechi in the eye. He dressed his lashes and held his head high. He ceased to go to school anymore, for the other children were embarrassed to be counted as friends.

Within a week or so Adene returned to her sunny and cheerful self, and this Zechi did not begrudge. She was only six, after all. He, however, was shamed.

He took no apprenticeship in trade, and his father ostracized him for this failure every day, muttering over his bowl of soup as his mother begged him to try again. Zechi listened with deaf ears, and stopped talking altogether, living within his own young saddened mind.

Without being asked he took the chore of carrying the buckets from the river to the crops, his jaw firmly set. He carried dozens of buckets every day, his arms growing stiff and sore, and later, strengthened. Every drop he spilled during these daily labors was to him as though he bled out his heart for tears.

His only joy was in the weekly treks he took to see Jayna, often leaving home long before the sun was up, and returning at dusk on some day or other. He refused to answer his parent's endless questioning, even when they swore time and again that they would wash their hands of him.

He began to carry a pack of supplies with him when he went, food and a blanket roll, and extra socks. Always extra socks.

Jayna made him strong, or at least planted the seeds that would grow to strength later. He still remained the sallow whimpering lad that he ever was, likely to cry in the hottest of moments.

This sadness left him pale in color, so that his parents told any who asked, "he is suffering from an internal illness, for which we can find no cure."

Many months passed.

The Dryad became his dearest friend, and he relished the manner in which she cared for the Deep Forest. He shared in the love she had for it.

"Jayna?"

He sat in the sun on his blanket roll by the small clearing, eating his lunch as they spoke of all that came to mind.

"How big is the world, Jayna? I should think I would like to see it." He took a large bite of a crisp apple.

She laughed, her attitude always somewhat cheered at his presence. "The world is vast enough to flood your life with adventure and surprises, my friend. But be assured, it is smaller than it seems."

"Do you think I should leave my home? Maybe explore a part of it?" His eyes lowered themselves to the ground. "Perhaps if I left, there would be some spine to me."

"Zechi, you possess a strong spirit. And you are very young. Wait a while, and be obedient to your

110

*elders. When the time comes, you will know it, and
you will become great."*

"Will I travel?"

*She smiled. "Yes. You will travel. And don't let a
one tell you no. When you are ready, you will know
it, and not a soul can stop you."*

*His thoughts lingered that night upon Jayna's
wise words, and an idea heated his heart from
within. He became eager, too eager to sleep, so he
took up his pack and left her meadow without a
word.*

*Dawn found him above the Odel Valley, seeking
out the herds of wild horses that roamed the land,
foraging for food. Sure enough, by evening he had
found them, and he followed the horses from a short
distance for the entire span of the sun, and he
learned their ways.*

*Through the night they each slept a mere hour in
shifts before waking to graze. They made their way
down to the valley, keeping a safe distance from the
village. They grazed here until just before the sun
rose, and they must flee before Men.*

*The herd trotted along the road to Toten Town,
cutting through the forest to the Longest River.
Here they would loiter about the watering hole for a
large part of the day where they would drink, graze
and nap in the sun. It was a mere mile from the
village.*

*The watering hole was the place. It was the only
spot they visited consistently, and the surrounding
area was large enough for what he planned.*

*He kept up with their movements with difficulty,
but it was worth it. He cast about for some lengths*

of rope he knew he would need, and he headed back to Toten Town one sunset. He returned immediately.

At times the herd noticed his presence, or smelled him on the wind. Their ears would perk up, and they would stare with wide eyes. But after a handful of days they seemed to perceive no threat from him, and when he'd returned from home with the ropes he needed he spent another two days following from a distance.

He was close to them now, close enough that the foals would come and sniff his extended hand, guarded by the careful strides of their mothers, who watched him warily.

Zechi spoke and sang to them all day, every day, and over the days that passed he picked out the two who had escaped from the corral at Adene's hand. He saw that he liked them for their thickness of coat and body, as they looked healthy and well fed. Though the black mare had been worked with when she was young, it would be a challenge, especially with them both being skeptical of men now. The one thing he had in his favor was this mare's early handling. She would remember his cues. Thus he made his plan slowly and carefully.

One early morning he walked with them to their watering hole, ropes knotted and ready. He figured he would start with the black one first, the mother.

When all had settled in to have a drink, each in their turn, he approached the black mare at her shoulder. Her long, dark neck stretched down to the river bank, the hair fringing across her neckline, the fur shiny. She looked up at him and he took one step back. He stood completely still until she returned to her water. Her bronze foal drank on the other side of her.

The old words of his many lessons with Miri echoed in his mind: "Where the head goes, the body will follow..."

He moved gently, causing her to raise her head again, and he lightly draped the loop around her neck. The mare started and pulled away, spooking the rest of the herd, who scattered. The black mare circled around him to follow them, then feeling the pressure of the loop she panicked, rearing up to her full height to free herself.

She pivoted on her haunches and spun away, pulling him over. He hit the ground hard and watched the herd run away, his mare trailing the rope behind her. He smiled from the ground as the dust clouded and settled.

With nothing more than a scraped elbow, Zechi was back the next day. He walked the herd down, relaxed nearby and remained as unthreatening as possible. By the following day he was able to approach again and take hold of the mare's fluttering rope. This time he was ready.

He shortened up on the rope, petting her shoulder, keeping her nose dipped towards him. She could only circle about. He kept their movements calm, so as not to upset and cause the herd to flee. He pet her on the shoulder at every opportunity. After some time she relaxed enough to graze, and he let her, guiding her from place to place, her foal following closely nearby.

After a time he set her free and returned the next day to catch her again. It was easier this time, and he led her to a rock and climbed aboard her broad back. The mare moved to the right, unsure. He asked nothing of her, only that she not throw him off.

He quieted his movements, and they rejoined the herd. He rode astride her all day and night, a quiet passenger. By morning the herd moved back to the watering hole, walking along the roadside. He allowed the mare to walk and trot as she pleased until she seemed to accept him on her back. Her foal kept pace right alongside her mother without question. He dismounted and arranged his loops so that a smaller loop sat around her nose. Remounting, he directed his ride away from the herd. The trio rode on to Toten Town.

When he came into the village people began to murmur and talk amongst themselves as they gathered on the road. He ignored them and rode on straight through to his house.

Harlkene was just leaving the house when Zechi called out to him, "open the gate!" Adene appeared in the doorway, her face curious.

Without a word Harlkene opened the mended corral, and Zechi rode them in. He dismounted and removed the ropes. These he handed to his father as he exited the corral.

"I will tell Nia," Harlkene said with obvious pride, and Zechi grinned, for he could already see the silver-haired woman watching him from across the path. The excitement built up inside him, and he felt as though he would burst for joy.

"I have one I must tell myself!" he cried, and he ran off into the woods, weary and hungry though he was.

₪

Jayna. He must tell Jayna. He smiled, sure that she would be proud of him, and he hurried on through the woods. He had been jogging briskly for almost half an hour when he heard a slight noise behind him.

He slowed to a walk, wondering if someone was there. He stopped his steps quite suddenly, and sure enough, he heard the muffled padding of footsteps behind him.

Zechi veered off to the river and waded across in a spot he knew to be shallow. Out of the corner of his eye he glanced down the bank at the same, murky swimming hole that he had once fallen into himself, unawares. Indeed, the marker he had left was still there.

He walked onto the opposite bank and disappeared into the trees before ducking behind one. A twig snapped and Zechi peeked out from his hiding spot as a small form emerged. To his surprise, it was Adene who appeared between the trees, a fresh white apron over her pink robes and matching ribbons in her hair.

"Adene!" he called out furiously, scrambling out from behind the bushes. He was surprised at himself that he could sound that angry. "No. Absolutely not. Go home!"

"I... I wanted to see where you go," she said softly, her soft blue eyes brimming with tears. Zechi found it hard to be mad at her. He sighed.

"I've been spending time in the woods. I enjoy it, all right? That is all. Now please, go home!"

"But you're over there!" she cried, pointing at the river between them, her pink face flushed at such a scandal. She had one foot resting on the fallen log. "It is forbidden!"

"All that is over here are trees. There is nothing else. Please, just go."

But another person emerged from the trees behind Adene, a tall, lean figure dressed in purple. His heart sank.

"So this is what you've been doing, boy!" Nia called out above the gurgle of the river. She pointed one long, silver fingernail in his direction. "Adene, go home!" she commanded. Her eyes were gray and cold.

But his sister stood there, whining, "I want to go with Zechi!"

Nia whipped around and snatched Adene by the arm, shaking her soundly. "You are too young to understand this!"

"Let go of her!"

Nia thrust out her cane and Adene tumbled to the ground. "My quarrel is not with your sister, but with yourself, you cretin. You are a shame to the clan!"

"What is wrong with my brother?" Adene looked scared and worried.

"Go home!" Zechi and Nia shouted in unison, then they glared at each other.

116

*"How did you find me?" he challenged. He was
actually curious to know.*

*"I saw your sister sneak after you this morning,
and I followed her. Come back, boy. You are
already in great trouble for crossing the divide.
Your parents' disappointment will be magnified
tenfold." She sounded triumphant in her words and
Zechi felt sick. His eyes caught a flash of pink and
Adene was plunging into the river.*

*"No!" he cried, and he all but saw her sink into
the hole.*

*He dropped his pack and leapt in after her,
swimming for all he was worth. The water was
murky, but his sister showed brightly enough and he
was able to wrap one strong arm around her waist
and bring her to the surface.*

*Nia dropped her cane and was hovering over the
riverbed. Together they dragged and pushed the girl
from the water.*

*Zechi crawled onto the shore after her, and he
could already see the look of despair on Nia's face.*

*"No," he whispered, his face stricken. He
grabbed the girl's shoulders. "Adene? Adene!" He
leaned over her body in disbelief. Her fair skin was
pure white, her face serene.*

She was gone.

ℿ

*He carried his sister back to Toten Town, his
face dirty and tear streaked and as set as stone. Nia
silently retrieved her cane and followed silently
behind him, thinking, no doubt, of the blame to be*

placed upon him. When she tried to help him carry,
he pulled his sister away.

When they reached the fringes of the village,
people began following them, asking questions and
whispering their wonder. He walked, solid as a
statue, and gently set her body in the town square.
He waited, his heart cold, as his parents forced
themselves through the crowd. Miri fell to her knees
and began to wail and Zechi's father stared, his
expression numb with shock.

The near silence was broken by Nia's bold
proclamation.

"This boy has brought destruction upon this
village, his family! He has even gone so far as to
corrupt his younger sister into following him across
the river, into the Unknown World, where she has
drowned!" She waved her arms around theatrically,
and the crowd gasped.

"That is right," she confirmed smoothly, "he has
broken the Nigh Law, willingly and knowingly. It is
his fault that this young one now lies dead."

"What is his punishment?" a patron called out
from the crowd. Everyone looked at Zechi. He
wanted to speak, but his throat was tight and thick
and he choked.

Nia's stare hardened, her eyes closing with
finality. "He will live with what he has done. That is
his punishment."

Zechi dropped his head and stared at Adene's
body through blurred tears. He dug into his pocket
and dropped the carven horse into her open hand.
"I'm sorry," he whispered, choking on his words.

And Zechi ran again.

௬

"Jayna!"

Zechi came tearing through the trees, his face covered in a blanket of distress, the pain very apparent.

"What is it, my child?" she asked, calm even in light of his uncontrollable despair.

Between sobs he told her what had happened. He had never cried so much in his entire life, scarcely accepting the fact that Adene, his precious little sister was... was... He began to moan, his eyes and nose pouring water.

"Zechi," Jayna said softly, and he looked up at her with large, watery eyes.

"Yes, my mother?"

"It was not your fault."

"Yes, my mother." He bowed his head yet again.

"Zechi, you are to come to me no longer."

His head snapped up. "W-what? Why?" His lip quivered, and his eyes flooded with fresh, warm tears.

"It is time for us to part ways for now. The world is unfolding as it should. Great things will be headed your way very soon."

"What? What will happen?" His face crumpled and he felt so alone.

She smiled sadly. "There is nothing to know. You must wait. You will know it when it is plain to see. It will be the beginning of a spiral of events that will lead you back to my boughs in many, many years from now."

"I will miss you."

"You can always speak to me through the trees, my friend."

"I can? How do I do this?" he cried, desperate.

"There is a tree in the corner by the corral near your home. Her name is Sounet, and she is eager to meet you. Place your hands upon her and you can speak to her, and she will speak to me."

"Thank you." He knew the tree of which she spoke.

He could hardly express his gratitude at this time when his heart felt as though it would be strangled within his breast. He left her then, a broken child, but filled with a distant hope that somehow, someday, all would be well.

He returned to his parents' home the following day and lived there without a word upon his tongue, and they avoided him as well. He went no more into the Deep Forest.

Within the year the soldiers came and killed his parents, whom he still loved, despite the rift between them. When they took his house he slept in the corner of the corral. He stayed near his dearest friend Sounet, waiting...

Nia watched him suspiciously always, knowing he did some evil when he lay his hands upon the tree. He ignored her. He remained on his own, a silent village pariah, still only a boy, quiet and sad until the day came that a girl wandered into his village. He saw her place her hands upon Sounet, her lips moving, and he knew that there was another who could speak to the trees.

The girl spoke of magical creatures and lore, and Zechi was shy when she approached him, and denied such talk, thinking of Jayna and the promise he swore to her.

Nia cornered her, and shortly after a wave of water overtook the village. The girl pulled him to safety among Sounet's branches.

It wasn't long until the yearly earthquake came and a giant creature ravaged their village in the night... Zechi clung to Sounet's trunk, terrified. He saw the girl called Deiji again. After the creature had passed through, the continents had reunited, the village ruined... He met the Dolphin Arill who told him to leave Toten Town and seek out the King of the Nigh Court... and Zechi found himself witness to the Odel Mountain War. He followed General Morim back to the Nigh Court where Mangiat was made king...

It was still many years before things got better.

Chapter Eight
The Dragons

PRESENT DAY

THE DRAGON

Geo flew high above the Eastern Ranges, keeping a close lookout for any who travelled below him. He had been searching for Deiji for three days, ever since the wind from the storm had carried him away.

He had awakened sore and tired, floating in the middle of the Southern Gale. He flew north at once. When he could not find his friend, he moved towards Mount Odel, an ache in his scaly breast; an ache brought on by the notion of an entire world before him in which to search, and nowhere to begin.

Knowing his fierce companion, she wouldn't give up the search for Mowat, so going to their Island or back to the Nigh court would be pointless.

He searched the seas, and while he did find the occasional ship, none were his girl. Though he knew he was too late, he flew over Toten Town and back to Mount Odel, hoping to find her, forgetting they were ever sore at one another.

Once near Odel, he saw a strange sight far below, on the side of the stream that had once been called the Unknown World. It was a little army of man, assembling themselves into rows, an odd sight at this time of supposed peace. Deiji had proudly told him that Mangiat mobilized no troops during his reign.

He continued on, hoping Deiji would be on Odel Mountain.

He had hardly been over the land an hour when he saw a sight that made his sore heart leap. A Dragon! There was another Dragon in the air - she was blue and flew quite gracefully. She was different than he. She wore planks of armor over her back and tail. A helmet covered most of her head, and even her legs wore guards.

The only time he had seen other Dragons had been during his training on the northernmost of the Dragon Islands. It had been nice, he decided, and he was always hopeful that one day he might live among his own kind. At times he felt ill of separation from his brethren, but he had Deiji and that was enough.

Geo blinked his large green eyes with wonder as the blue armored Dragon flew in his direction. She suddenly changed her course, lifting one slender wing to the sky and spiraling down to the ground.

Watching these movements, he knew she noticed him, too.

He sped up and flew alongside her, wary of her wingspan. She peered sideways at him with a smirk before folding her wings into a dive and dropping out of sight.

He dove after her, transfixed. Her thin blue flank was studded with shiny blue pearls, and her tail was long, ending in a narrow double-edged blade. Her talons were smaller and finer than his own, but they were *so* blue…

She changed directions sharply again and rose into the open sky, the air from her powerfully beating wings sending him off balance. Geo gave her a dopey grin and tried to get closer, and the Dragon nipped at his neck with her strong jaws, though he noticed that she did not use her teeth.

Determined, he swooped below her and turned belly up. They locked talons and began fighting furiously, nipping and knocking each other with the flats of their tail blades as they fluttered to the ground.

They tumbled into the dust together in a colorful flurry of lake green and ocean blue. Geo shook his whole body as they broke apart and stepped back, breathing hard. They had only just taken a full look at one another when a light haired man came running up the path, out of breath.

"River!" he panted, "I told you to keep watch! Who..?" He stopped when he saw Geo, and a cheery grin spread across his face. "Geo!" He approached him with open arms, and Geo gladly lifted one scaly arm for a hug.

It was Docin, the Dragon Keeper he had tutored under after he left the Island and Deiji. He had learned so much from this man, and it was good to see a dear friend.

"I see you have met my companion," the Keeper motioned towards the beautiful blue River, who was watching them proudly. Her jaw was strong, her eyes soft and intelligent, and Geo nodded eagerly in agreement, sitting up as straight as he could.

"River, this is Geo, an old student of mine."

His green eyes met her glowing blue ones and they both nodded curtly, though her smile was sly and warm. He wanted to play with her again, and the longing was difficult to control.

"Maybe you can help me, Geo," Docin suggested slowly. Geo listened intently as his Teacher explained what he was looking for, a special Rune. He frowned.

Docin's eyes shown with an eagerness he had never seen before. "You know where it is," he hissed greedily. It was not a question. Geo shook his head, but Docin was not convinced. "Will you take me there?"

Before Geo could answer, a strong gust of wind rustled the trees and a cute little cat floated down from the heavens, landing right between them.

"Geo!" Puff Puff's voice echoed, and Docin was staring. Geo couldn't tell if he was impressed or merely amused. In any case, he took a step back.

"Geo, Deiji needs you right now!" she squeaked. "They've been overtaken by Pirates! Follow me!"

Geo rose into the air right away, and Docin rushed up to River, throwing one leg over her armored neck. "We're coming with you!" he shouted, and Geo paused, lost for words.

"Now, Geo!" Puff shouted earnestly.

He didn't nod, didn't shrug or give any hint of an answer. He flew away. And they followed.

₪

THE KEEPER OF FIRE

The ship was rocking. It was colder than it had been and was still dark. She opened her eyes, fully awake now. It took her a moment to remember where they were. She was stiff and moved slowly.

"We're here!" a Pirate called down to them gruffly, and Deiji could see his candle bobbing about in the darkness as he descended the ladder.

It was early the next morning and Zechi was still sleeping, his head rested stiffly against her shoulder.

"All hands! All hands on deck!" she could hear the distant call.

"Zechi." She moved his shoulder gently. "Get up."

"Mmm?"

"We're leaving."

"Ah." He rose to his feet, and she could hear him yawning.

The Pirate unlocked the brig. "All right, walk. You, boy, in front. No talking."

He prodded them each in the back with a blunt object, ushering them onto the deck. The daylight was bright when they emerged, and Deiji's eyes closed involuntarily to the shock of it. Her eyelids fluttered as they adjusted. She squinted and could see they were just off the shore of her Island. She looked around and saw Mangiat, still tied to the mast, looking very tired and nervous.

The crew had gathered and Micid stood apart, beside the Captain. Deiji felt a tight burning deep in her soul at the sight of Micid standing there looking so smug. Well, the woman wasn't going to get away with it, she decided.

"Micid has requested a special audience with her niece," Captain Farlane announced. The beginnings of a smile tugged on the corners of his mouth. "It is her wish that Deiji, er, walk the plank."

A cheer rose up from the men and Deiji stifled the urge to roll her eyes. She glanced at Mangiat who looked mildly concerned. She could hardly feign fear. "Oh. Please don't." She furrowed her brow and tried to look afraid. She could hear Zechi snort in amusement beside her.

"Send her overboard!" Micid roared, and the men pointed their swords and knives at her, crowding in, urging her towards the plank that led to the open reef.

Ruan leaned in and hissed through broken teeth, "we be here for the treasure, lass, and if ye be lyin' your friends will meet th' same end, or worse."

Deiji ignored him. She looked to her Aunt who was accepting a dagger from the Captain and caught her eye. "We are not done here," she said scathingly, and she was pleased when Micid paled some.

"On with it!" Farlane hollered, and one of his men lunged with his sword fully extended, and

Deiji leapt into the water with a foamy splash. She transformed instantly into her Mermaid form and swam under the hull. There was someone in the water nearby, and it wasn't long until Arill swam up beside her.

"What in the name of the ocean has been going on?" He was very irritated.

She opened her mouth to explain as *The Lantern* dropped four lifeboats into the water, and they watched the ripples fan out until they faded.

"We were overtaken by Pirates." She hastily gave an account of all that had unfolded. The Dolphin stared at her, astounded.

"Why did you not stop it, then?" They swam after the boats.

"What do you mean? How could I have?"

"You know what you are," Arill called over with a note of finality. "If you so wished it, it would have been stopped. You could have escaped."

"I feared for Zechi and Mangiat... They are innocent and, essentially, powerless. I could not risk their lives."

"You could have paused the frame of time itself, or fought them off with magic. You are far more powerful than they are."

Deiji felt uncomfortable. "I don't know if I could attack them. After all, I *am* much more powerful than they are. I don't want to, um..." She stumbled over her words. "Kill," she finished. "Again," she added, thinking of the Stie called Anaou and the battle of Mount Odel.

"Never be afraid to use your magic, Jai. You are far overdue for becoming what you already are!

There is no reason to hesitate. No reason at all. Deiji, you make me angry!" And indeed the Dolphin looked angry, his normally calm eyes blazing red.

"I… I will try," she answered lamely. She frowned, suddenly feeling defensive. "Don't forget that I am still learning," she cried out with more anger than she intended. "I am still new at this." She glared at the Dolphin defensively.

Arill smiled. "You need to be more assertive, is all. Take control of the situation by utilizing your abilities. It will come to you in time," he said permissively. "For now, we need to focus on undoing all of this." Arill looked at the surface apprehensively. "I'm going to breach! See who is where."

He flew up and back into the water with a splash of frothy bubbles that still clung to his body. "Zechi is in a lifeboat with them. Looks like Mangiat must still be back on the ship."

"Then we shall have to save him!"

₪

THE KING

"Stand still, you filthy Centaur!"

He struggled against his bonds, despite his chaffed wrists. Micid was shouting at him. Two men jumped forward and tightened the ropes painfully behind the mast. His head was pounding from the sun and his thirst. His tongue was dry and his arms were sore from being tied through the chill of an entire night.

Deiji was safe he knew, but he was most concerned for Zechi, who they had taken, bound and gagged, onto the Island. A fair amount of sailors had been left behind on the ship, as well as Micid, who appeared to bear some sort of authority in the Captain's absence.

She leaned in close to him and Mangiat recoiled; the sun and sea had taken their toll on this woman. Her skin was as brown and wrinkled as faded leather, her skin cracked in places, hardened by the salt on the wind.

"Hope you're not too worried about your friend," she smirked, pulling her lips back to reveal brown-stained teeth. Mangiat tried to show no emotion. Deiji had told him little of Micid's treatment of her as a child, but he knew enough to loathe the woman completely.

Micid gazed off at the Island, and he could see a peek of it between the rails. It was a small island, and he could see a jumble of rocky hills rising up from its center. The reef was enshrouded in a heavy mist that sat thick upon the water. Micid sighed longingly and gazed at the Captain's dagger.

"Does the Captain love you?" he asked shortly, and Micid spun around.

"What's that?" she said sharply.

He shrugged. "The Captain… There seems to be something between the two of you. I only wondered…"

"Well cease to wonder, you filthy beast!" She looked back over the water. "He will realize what I am someday. I am still among his most trusted men," she added loftily.

"So you're a man, are you?" He smiled at his own wit, and Micid leaned in close and hissed, "when they get back you are next to walk, my friend. And that boy's sapphires are *mine*."

Mangiat looked away, containing his anger easily. It could not be long now...

Sure enough, as Micid opened her cracked lips to speak again, a voice cried out, "get away from him!" Deiji's face appeared over the ladder.

"Well, if it isn't my brother's brat," Micid drawled, but Deiji's angry voice cut her words before she could say more.

"You are not good enough to call my father family," she spat. She pointed her fingers at Mangiat. "*Sieolga!*"

He flinched but found his hands suddenly freed. He slowly brought his arms around, trying not to cry out at the stiffness and pain.

"Get in the lifeboat, Mangiat," she directed him, not taking her fiery eyes away from Micid or the crew that was inching towards her.

He obeyed, stepping gingerly into the lifeboat that hung over the side, ready to launch.

"*Azioni!*" She threw a hand his way and the ropes unreeled themselves at a sickening pace. He fell into the ocean with a large splash, and clung desperately to the lifeboat's sides, dizzy. Arill appeared immediately and began to push him away from *The Lantern*.

There was a splash behind him and he knew Deiji was safe. She joined Arill and lifted her head from the waves.

"*Cascata!*" she cried, and an enormous wave of twisting blue water rose high and crashed into the ship, utterly capsizing it. He saw Micid's frightened face clinging to the ratlines as the men scurried about for a brief moment before being overtaken by the sea. He looked away.

"Are you okay?" Deiji looked up at him from the water as they moved quickly to the shore.

He nodded. "Thank you."

They pushed his boat to the beach where the other lifeboats waited, sprawled across the sand, lassoed to saplings. Mangiat jumped out as soon as they touched land, and Deiji came out of the water after bidding a quick farewell to the annoyed Dolphin.

"Let us then find the others!" she called back to him as she raced past, her wet, dark hair flying out behind her.

He stopped a moment, ignoring his headache, a wave of courage welling up inside his breast.

"Jai!" he called out with conviction.

"Yes." She turned back to face him.

"You know you're beautiful, don't you?"

She grinned. "Thank you, Mangiat."

They ran.

ו

He slunk low to the sand beside Deiji as they neared the Pirates, though they still managed to move quickly. He whispered, "Jai, I only just realized... I have lost my books! My tonic! All was on the ship. I -"

"Don't worry," she hissed back at him. "Puff has everything, and she will come soon. Now, do you see anything?"

"No, nothing." He felt relieved. They continued their low sprinting across the beginnings of the forest jungle and he heard Deiji chuckle. He looked over at her. "What is it?"

"This is the same path I once wandered the time I found Geo."

He nodded absentmindedly and stared at the trees curiously. It was stiflingly hot here in the jungle, humid and with no cooling breezes. The obnoxious chatter of birds and other animals was a surprise to Mangiat, as his only experience of the forest was that of the subdued mainland. The jungle here was alive with bright colors and many different heights and types of trees. So this was where Deiji lived.

Soon they saw the Dragon Keep, the cave which sat bright and shimmering as the afternoon sun poured in. They slowed pace, quieted their steps.

"I hear voices," Mangiat whispered, his Centaur's ears better attuned to the forest. They crouched even lower and picked their way to the cave's entrance and peeked around the rocky edge.

Half a dozen men were bent over, rifling through the mounds of gold and jewels and silver. Captain Farlane was examining the far corners of the cave, looking down as if into some hole. In his hand was a length of rope, which he could see led to Zechi's bound wrists. The boy was struggling silently and Mangiat nearly laughed.

His heart began to flutter, and he concentrated on breathing evenly. "Don't make yourself ill," he berated himself silently. He must focus.

"What?"

"Nothing," he answered her quickly, and they pulled back out of sight. "What do we do?"

"I could attack them, only I don't want to harm Zechi."

"Deiji, you are powerful enough to stop this."

She smiled plainly. "So I am told. But I am not experienced enough."

POOF! A small cat made of cloud appeared at Deiji's side, startling them both.

"Puff Puff!"

"My Master, I went straight to Geo yesterday, and he is just approaching the edge of the Island. He comes any moment now. Two creatures have leeched onto him; a man and a blue Dragon." She sat back and nibbled one leg, as if chasing a flea.

Mangiat and Deiji exchanged glances. Deiji looked back to her cat.

"Puff, I want you to become a Dragon yourself, right now – a red one. Go in the cave and save Zechi. You are to be sure that he comes to no harm," she added with warning.

Puff nodded airily and began to grow and change color. Two Dragons descended from the sky.

"Geo!" Deiji shouted loudly at his green form. Geo landed beside her and they fell into a cheerful embrace. "I'm glad you're here," Mangiat heard her whisper. He felt a rush of sorrow and happiness in their reunion. This was good. He glanced to the cave, certain they were no longer secret.

Sure enough, men began to rush out of the cave, weapons in hand. He had to laugh as their angry, weathered faces turned white with fear at the sight of the three monstrous Dragons that stood waiting for them, their teeth bared, their eyes maddened. Docin slid off the back of his Dragon and drew his dagger.

"Well, this will be over soon," Mangiat said loudly, feeling giddy. Most of the men retreated back into the cave; two tried to run.

"Round them up!" Deiji cried out. "But spare their lives, if you can."

River swooped into the cave, a simple smile of pleasure on her scaly face as she herded two men of the into the far corner, leaving them trapped and shaking. Geo chased after two who tried to escape into the jungle. He grabbed one with his massive talons and held down another with his hind leg before snatching him up into his mouth.

There was a loud bellow of anguish from inside the cave, and Puff ran in to where River sat guarding her prisoners. Mangiat galloped after her, but she had stopped.

"Deiji," Puff called out cautiously, waving her red spiked tail, "we may have a problem."

Mangiat pushed past her bulky form as Deiji came up behind him. He sucked in his breath sharply. Everyone froze.

Captain Farlane stood against the far wall, his cutlass held steadily against Zechi's throat.

ฏ

He groaned inwardly. Zechi! Of all those whom he wished to protect…

"I am sorry, Master," Puff apologized.

The Captain moved and everyone jolted, but he was only backing away.

Deiji spoke, and he suddenly felt at ease. If anyone had power and control over this situation, it was Jai.

"Puff," she whispered sternly, not taking her eyes from the Captain's inching movements, "he is going underground. Join to me. We're going Centaur."

Puff immediately complied and began to shrink, the Pirates howling of witchcraft as she hovered above Deiji's body before melting into her. Swirls of cloud twisted around the girl's body until she was Centaur once more.

"Dragons!" Deiji's voice rose loud enough for all to hear. "Keep these men immobile and wait for our return. Mangiat, you are coming with me."

His heart swelled with pride above anger and he could all but keep himself contained as Farlane and Zechi fell further into shadow.

"Let's go!" she cried with spirit, and Mangiat reared up in the excitement, and they both lunged forward. The Captain broke into a run, pushing a stumbling Zechi ahead of him, and they disappeared from sight.

"*Dae!*" A bubble of light hovered above Deiji's face and seemed to flood the direction in which she looked whenever she moved. It was cold down here, colder than he expected it to be, out of the sticky humidity of the jungle.

"What's down here?" he called to the girl as they galloped down the steep hole.

"Tunnels," she called back grimly, her voice echoing through the darkness. "Lots of tunnels."

"Great."

"It splits off up here! Stay with me; you don't want to get lost."

There was no sign of the Captain or the boy, and his hopes took a deep dive as he saw the sudden split ahead. Now they had two tunnels.

"Which way?" He felt helpless. They paused and listened for sounds, but all that came was the steady drip-drip echoing throughout the cavern.

"To the right!" She pointed to a footprint in the dust, a scuff in the gravel. It wasn't long until the cave split off again, this time into three narrow tunnels.

"Well?" His voice was high. They had both stopped and were on the verge of panic. "Zechi!" Mangiat called, his voice echoing away. There was a muffled shout in reply, but they could not tell from which way it came.

"Oh, this is like a nightmare," he groaned.

"Look!" Deiji snatched something up from amidst the rocks and rubble. She dropped it in his hand.

"A Sapphire!"

"To the left!"

They ran a little ways longer and came to a junction where another tunnel joined to theirs, and they could go right or left as well.

"There!" Mangiat shouted in relief, for there was the Captain, boy in tow, trying to go to the right.

The Captain turned, holding Zechi as a shield. "I will kill him," he promised scathingly.

"Zechi, duck!" Deiji shouted, then, "*Ferula Debeo!*" Zechi crumpled and a haze of silver fire flew at the Captain. It struck him square and he fell, stunned, on top of the boy.

Mangiat rushed to the boy's side and shoved the burnt Captain away. He untied him quickly, pulling him into a tight embrace.

"Get up," Deiji growled at the fallen Pirate, nudging him with her foot.

Mangiat tossed the length of cut rope to her, then turned back to Zechi.

"GET UP!" Deiji roared, and she kicked his quiet form. Farlane groaned. She fell into a flurry of kicking and cursing, circling him, shouting words of hate. Mangiat glanced over and opened his mouth but didn't know what to say.

"Really, I'm fine," Zechi was insisting, though he looked happy that Mangiat cared so.

"Scum! *Heiechi!* You will walk to your fate, fool!" She pointed her open palm towards the Captain's face.

"ENOUGH!" Mangiat roared.

Deiji looked up, genuinely surprised. "You would let this man live?"

Mangiat shook his head. "It is not our place to say. Not even yours." He turned back to the boy and avoided her gaze. It was quiet. "You dropped this," Mangiat said with a smile, holding out the Sapphire.

"Thank you. I snuck this one into my mouth before we were tied up."

"Where is the bag now?"

"He has them." Zechi nodded towards the fallen Captain.

Mangiat stood up swiftly. "Where are they? Give them to me!" Deiji stepped back.

Farlane coughed, his hair and jacket singed, and he motioned to his waistband.

Mangiat knelt and snatched them away angrily. He handed them back to Zechi, who promptly added the stray Sapphire and tucked them safely away.

"Get him up," Deiji directed. "Let's get back to the others."

ℿ

Back at the cave, Mangiat was both pleased and relieved to see Geo and River standing guard over the Pirates. Not a one had escaped. Docin crouched nearby building a fire.

He couldn't help but notice the look on Geo's face as he stared at the Dragon called River. He smiled inwardly, happy for his friend, who was obviously smitten.

When the captured Captain was added to his men he fell limply onto his side and lay there, unmoving. Mangiat stared at them. "What should we do with them?" he asked aloud.

"Well I certainly do not want them on my Island," Deiji scoffed.

"Should we let them live?" he asked carefully, then the Captain started choking.

He began to convulse, a very crude and ugly movement, and Mangiat was stricken with fear, although he cared nothing for the man.

Ruan cried from where he was bound, "he is dying!"

"Save him!" another cried.

"Jai?" He looked helplessly at his friend.

Deiji dropped to her knees beside Farlane. She seemed to consider the panicked faces of those around her. Ruan dropped to his knees at her side, his hands bound behind his back. His plea was simple. "Please."

After a moment, she placed her hands upon the Captain's charred flesh and whispered, "*Hertzel*."

A soft glow emanated from her fingertips and spread across the man's' wounds. The charred flesh became whole, the burns clear again. The Pirates stared on in awe as their Captain ceased to writhe about and sat up. He stared at the girl in shock.

The man slowly rose to his feet and Jai met his pace. He looked down at his body, examining his hands and arms in wonder. They stood there, gazing at one another. It seemed as though everyone held their breath as these two foes stood motionless.

Then Captain Farlane bowed. And Deiji bowed in return as the men cheered.

ℼ

All the men were released and they made camp together, though they remained leery of the two Dragons.

"Where are you going on this journey of yours?" Docin asked them. Deiji and Mangiat quickly launched into the tale of their search for Mowat, and even Farlane listened intently.

"I dun understand any o' this," Ruan spoke up. "Where did ye come from?"

Mangiat stared right back at him, arms folded. "Where did *you* come from? I was certain that Man only lived on the Eastern shore. Yet here you are, on the far side of the Western world. How can this be?"

Docin cleared his throat and tucked a thin braid of white hair behind his ear, and the gathering looked up in interest.

"Perhaps we should sit and talk of things. I am certain we all have questions for one another." He clasped his pale hands together.

Mangiat glanced at Deiji, who nodded. He still did not like nor trust this Dragon Keeper. Everyone joined them, huddling in closely around the fire.

"The Pirates of the Western Sea were of the first of Man to cross the divide that once existed between the two continents," Docin began.

"Shall we eat?" Mangiat interrupted. "Share such a tale over a meal, perhaps?"

"I'm on it," Deiji proclaimed, and the men gathered around the fire, as eager as small children. "Puff! Fish for nine, please. And for two Dragons. And please inform Arill that all is well." The cat disappeared with a puff, and Mangiat looked back to Docin, surprised to see him gazing peacefully at Deiji. He frowned.

Docin continued, "two hundred forty-four years ago, after Man emerged from the sea, they settled down across the eastern half of the world, driving the Mystical creatures to the western half, including the Dragons who fled further to the Islands. For many years Man and Mystical lived on these two halves, separated by what used to be the Longest River. Almost one hundred years later, a small group of men and women, claiming the Nigh laws were unjust, protested by packing up their caravan and leaving."

"The predecessors of the Toten Town villagers," Zechi cut in from the shadow of the trees. Everyone looked at him in surprise.

"That's right," said Docin, impressed. "Nomadic folk. These soon-to-be settlers made it to a spot on the river bank which is now Toten Town. They made camp and discussed the crossing of the River. Most of them changed their minds and settled there, founding the town. A small band pressed on. They crossed the Longest River, and were labeled by the common public as barbarians, heathens. Social separatists.

"They made their way as nomads through the Deep Forest, and were eventually discovered and led by the Rabbits, who brought them to the Lost Marshes on the Western shore. Here they lived among the Pegasus for fifty years until they learned the ways of the stars and sea."

"That's us!" Ruan called out proudly, looking to his fellow pirates for confirmation. The men grinned and called out, "aye!"

Docin laughed. "By the time one hundred years had passed, they had built two solid ships and sailed from their shore and explored all the surrounding waters, attacking ships that carried explorers, eventually making the discovery of Islands to the north. They avoided the Islands to the south, however," his eyes sparkled, "for their deathly fear of Dragons."

The Pirates laughed loudly at this, for they were such as who loved a good tale.

"Bloodthirsty treasure mongerers, be Dragons!" a sailor called out, and the men roared and cheered.

Puff appeared with food for all and soon the air was filled with the sounds and smells of sizzling fish. They talked and ate and laughed together as night set on.

"How did you know of all this?" Deiji asked Docin shyly. He looked Deiji directly in the eyes and they both smiled. Mangiat decided he hated the man.

"I read books. Historical accounts written by scholars, the first few who could read and write." His white face brightened. "I have them in my home, on my Island. Perhaps you should come see them sometime. After all, we are neighbors of sorts."

Deiji's face flushed pink, her voice nearly a whisper. She brushed her long hair away from her neck. "Perhaps. And how are things with the Mermaids?" she asked quickly, changing the subject. "Any new developments since we last spoke?"

"I have not found the Rune yet... I think this is one quest I may very well fail at."

"Yes, Mermaids can be nasty creatures," Mangiat cut in, and he was surprised when Captain Farlane looked up from his food and laughed in seeming agreement.

Puff Puff floated to Mangiat's side and dumped a satchel at his feet. "Your books, my king." She gave him a sweet, affectionate smile.

Cheered, he opened his journal and scribbled away as one of the men produced a bottle of rum, passing it around as they ate. They took turns telling tales of lore by the fireside, outlandish tales that Mangiat could only smile at.

He glanced around through all the merrymaking, and saw Deiji close to Geo, whispering, apologizing. Zechi stood with his hands pressed against a tree, his eyes closed meditatively. Mangiat gazed to the heavens, to the stars that held the message to wait patiently.

He had just touched his head where the familiar pain was, when he felt a pair of eyes on him. He looked up to meet Deiji's steady gaze. She jerked her head to the side and stood up discreetly. He waited a moment before following her.

They met at the edge of the dark clearing, just barely into the jungle. He could hardly make out her silhouette in the starlight.

"What is it, milady?" He felt shy, and was somewhat grateful that the night masked his features.

"Mangiat…" she began softly, touching her fingertips to his cheek. He met her hand with his own, his stomach turning with nervousness. The noise and laughter from the campfire seemed suddenly loud and disruptive.

"Let's go somewhere else," Deiji suggested.

"Yes, let's," he agreed eagerly, and he cast about for a new path or direction.

"No," she said, putting a hand to his arm.

"But where?"

She closed her eyes, and Mangiat blinked. In just a fraction of a moment he found himself within a different realm.

Chapter Nine
The Rune

*H*e opened his eyes in shock. He was standing on nothing, surrounded by millions of the very stars he looked at each and every night. How he was suspended there, he did not know. But it wasn't his first visit to such a place.

A thin red light cut through the emptiness of space and Deiji was walking towards him, her hair long, loose and whipping about, as if on an invisible flow of wind. Her sari was clean, white, and it too fluttered.

It reminded him of his days as a student under Mowat, days when Mowat would take him out of the world and into his cave, the vast cave alight with stars… His heart gave a flip-flop when he realized that was exactly where he was. Only this time…

"Jai," he whispered.

She smiled and a sun of a distant world swung close in its orbit, sending its fine rays across her radiant face. Her dark eyes turned green when the sun hit them, a lovely emerald green.

"You changed your eyes."

She smiled. "I have always wanted green eyes."

He laughed, but it was a far off laugh, as if from a dream.

"Mangiat, I brought you here to discuss a few things. I thought we could use some privacy," she offered.

"Good. That is good. You haven't taken a liking to that Docin creature have you?" he blurted out, quite embarrassed.

She seemed to take no notice of this. "Oh, no. I feel a tad uneasy about the man. As if there is something he's not telling me. His soul holds a lie..." Her green eyes misted over and he could tell she thought of it.

"You had something to tell me?"

"Oh, yes," she snapped back to their time and space. "Yes, I wanted to speak to you."

"Say on."

"It concerns Zechi."

"And what of Zechi?"

"I have been watching him, for longer than we've all been here together these several days. When we first met in Toten Town, I saw his potential. Even on the Island we often spoke through the trees these last few years."

He raised his eyebrows. He did not know of this.

"My point is, I believe Zechi has incredible potential."

147

"As do I," he cut in quickly.

"Yes, and with that said, I was going to ask your permission to take him on as a student of sorts. You know, after all has been finished here, and after you think he has learned all he can from you."

His eyes widened. He had not thought of this! "That is a wonderful idea," he agreed. "He's all yours."

"Excellent." She smiled.

"Shall we return to the campfire, then?" He offered his arm, nervous to be alone with her in such a private setting.

"Well... I also wanted to inquire as to your health."

His eyes darkened and he looked down and studied one of his hooves.

She lowered her gaze a little, trying to catch his eye. "There's something you haven't been telling me, Mangiat."

"Yes, milady."

"What is it, then?" she asked softly. "Maybe I can help."

"I... I don't know."

"Mangiat, tell me." Her voice was quiet, but firm. Her eyes lovely and pressing.

He was quiet for a moment longer. He could feel tears brimming in his eyes and was then ashamed. She was suddenly close to him, her hand on his shoulder for comfort. She opened her mouth, but he spoke first, stumbling over his words, pouring it all out, his words plowing along faster than he could think them.

"Deiji... I am ill. Very ill. It started about a year into my kingship when I began to have headaches, so many headaches, and so painful, too! Doctors and herbalists could do nothing, and they worsened. Finally, a physician from the apothecary came to my aid with an herbal tonic. It keeps my pains at bay, but I still suffer temporary blindness at times. It is mostly just pain. And I cannot smell things sometimes. It was decided that I have a growth of some sort on the innards of my head, and it is said I have only two more years..." His voice trailed off and he was stunned to see that Jai was smiling.

He frowned. "Do you not see? Do you not understand? I –"

"Is that all? That is an easy fix."

"What?"

"Kneel. Close your eyes."

He obeyed, perplexed and excited at this idea of hope. She placed her hands on his head, her own bowed in deep concentration. He suddenly felt depressed. This wouldn't work, couldn't work. How foolish could he be? There were no miracles, not really. He closed his eyes to stop the tears.

Deiji did not hesitate. She smiled with great energy and cried out, "*HERTZEL!*" The same spell he had seen her use twice before. A great white light flashed through the vastness of space and beyond. The dull throb that Mangiat lived with every day for the last four years ceased at once.

"Jai!" His face was white with shock and pleasure. He was healed! He knew he was healed, knew it for sure. The sickness that had plagued his gut and left his neck inflamed day after day was gone. It was gone!

He scrambled to his feet and pulled her into a tight embrace, laughing and crying, nearly knocking her off her feet as he rocked her from side to side. She laughed loudly and they pulled apart.

"There is one more thing I must ask." She smiled shyly.

He clasped her hands in his, a large grin on his face. "Anything!" He felt dizzy in all the excitement, but it was not the feeling of illness. It was of renewal and of love. He looked at this beautiful creature and knew, truly knew...

"I want you to be my spouse."

ﬥ

Her spouse. Even as they returned to the campfire he was still alight with disbelief. Jayna had been Mowat's spouse. He had never heard their story, but he knew it had been an intense tale.

As spouses they would become partners, there to help one another along in all aspects of life and the world. He would be her helpmate; she would be his Queen. He shivered. It also brought with it the promise of immortal life, as she was the sacred Keeper. They could be with one another for one hundred years and more if they chose, for as long as they wished, until Jai relinquished the Rune of Life to another.

He could not stop smiling. He would be with her forever. And for him, to have awaited death so soon, to have it delayed, and then given the gift of eternal life… He figured he was in a dream.

They saw the campfire through the trees and Deiji laughed nervously a little. He looked over at her.

"What is it?"

"The Pirates." She laughed again, shaking her head. "I haven't told them that I sunk their ship!"

₪

SCRAPE. SCRAPE.

Mangiat woke beside the smoldering fire in the early morning's humidity. A few sailors were still dozing nearby, but he could hear Docin's voice, deep and intriguing. When Deiji responded with a laugh he woke fully with a start, and scrambled to his feet.

Geo and River were cuddled together, snoring, on the edge of the clearing. Zechi slept high above them in the branches of a tree. Deiji was sitting on a log nearby, sharpening her sword while Docin leaned against a sapling.

SCRAPE.

He approached the two rather nervously, wondering if last night had in fact, been a dream after all. His stomach was ice cold, and he was surprised when Deiji set her sword aside and greeted him warmly with a soft kiss on the cheek. She turned back to Docin, who had averted his eyes momentarily.

"Go on."

"As I was saying," he drawled, shooting an irritated look at the Centaur, "Geo has far more potential that you ever knew. He and Deiji could never communicate with words, you see," he looked at Mangiat, including him in the discussion. "There is a lot she might not know, as is the case with Geo's fire."

Mangiat frowned. "Geo has special fire?"

"Oh, yes. Geo was a fun one to train. He can choose his fire like any Dragon, of course. The fun one is the fireballs. He can shoot them, one after the other…" he smiled in nostalgia, his eyes on the treetops.

"He is a green Dragon, with poisonous claws and teeth – "

"But I know these things!" Deiji interjected, setting her sword sharpener down.

" – An Emerald Dragon, originally from the Deep Forest. That's where his kind lived until the invasion of Man caused a rush of Mystical creatures into their territory, which caused them to flee. What a disgusting part of Man's history," he added with a curled lip.

He continued. "Very private creatures, Dragons. More concerned about their Keeps, treasures and loyalties than much else. They were forced to a small group of Islands that aren't nearly large enough for their numbers and needs. And of course they mixed their blood once they all gathered on the Islands…" He looked at his pale fingernails distractedly.

"And what is this 'potential' you spoke of?" Mangiat asked impatiently. He did not like this haughty man at all!

" Ah, yes, that. See, Geo has this special ability seen rarely in his kind, and it proves he is a pureblooded Dragon!" Docin leaned forward as if revealing an incredible secret. "He can breathe onto plants – dead or dying – and revitalize them. That is his power. He has many abilities, mostly untapped, but he's honing them, steadily."

"I've seen it," Deiji whispered, entranced. Mangiat looked at her in surprise.

The Dragon Keeper gazed at her, his eyes lowering themselves down to her pendant. "Geo is not the only one with powerful abilities." Then he read aloud, *"Only in the darkness can you see the stars. Only here you will discover what you are. Reach beyond your daily fare; one day time will bring you there."*

Mangiat's heart began to pound with fear. He looked at Deiji, whose eyes had widened considerably.

"You… You can read the inscription?" she sputtered in awe. Mangiat knew it was no good, the man obviously knew what he was looking at. Docin knew it was the Rune. He braced himself for the fight that was sure to ensue.

"Oh, of course," Docin said loftily. "I know most of the older languages." His pale blue eyes were transfixed on the stone and its circular engravings. Deiji seemed frozen, lost for words.

Docin's eyes glittered with greed, and Deiji broke free from whatever held her. The man lunged at her. Mangiat drew his knife and jumped between them... He heard Deiji's panicked voice cry out *"Vorst Gel!"*

The world fell silent.

רן

THE KEEPER OF FIRE

Deiji was breathing quite heavily as the world around her stood motionless. She saw Docin hovering there in an awkward pose, one arm extended, fingers reaching for the Rune. Mangiat was in the air, his four black legs leaping between them, knife drawn and pointed at Docin. Hovering but never falling.

She looked around at the quiet jungle. River and Geo were just raising their heads to the commotion. The Pirates still lay asleep in the dirt, seemingly forever. The wispy smoke from the dying fire curled into the air and stayed there. Captain Farlane was drinking hot tea from a tin mug. He had fumbled the cup, and the tea was spilling. It was going to fall into his lap.

She frowned.

Deiji had only read of this spell, never tried it. She did not know how to reverse this spell, and thus make life continue. She groaned.

It had been a desperate move, she knew, but her mind had gone strangely blank when Docin made to attack her.

"Some warrior," she grumbled. She sighed and closed her eyes to go to the stars. Once she was within the fabric of space, she doubtfully called Arill into her presence. Would this work?

"There you are!" he called out in surprise as he appeared ahead of her, his body writhing as though still swimming. "What is going on *now*?"

She told him a brief version of the events, and he listened carefully.

"I used a spell to stop time, only I can't reverse it!" she finished.

"Oh, my." He indeed looked concerned. "Mowat has used that magic before, but he always managed to break the spell on his whim. Now, where is the Hourglass of Time?" He glanced around expectantly, but all there was around were the stars.

"I... I don't know," she answered lamely.

"Then how did you stop time?" The Dolphin was bewildered.

"I used the spell from the book, *The Keeper's Magic*. It worked."

Arill closed his gray eyes.

"What is it?" she asked anxiously.

"It's okay. It is okay. We just need to find the Hourglass, is all. You ought to have it in your possession anyway," he added, "being what you are."

She did not answer, but looked out into the void.

"Jai."

"Yes."

"I know we have all the time in the world at the moment," his eyes sparkled at his pun and she had to smile, "but we should go."

"Where to? Do you know where the Hourglass is?"

"No. But we shall search for it among the stars. It cannot be far." He swam ahead through the vastness of space, and Deiji followed.

They wove quickly in and out of the empty space that sat between the millions of suns and planets, and as she crossed over each swirl of galaxy, she found herself more and more astounded.

"Just how much is there to all this out here?" Jai asked carefully.

The Dolphin laughed. "It is never-ending, milady."

She frowned. "And exactly how much of it am I in charge of?"

He chuckled. "For now? Just set the balance of Nigh. The other worlds will wait for you. The time will come in many years hence when you will use the Hourglass of Time to do a thousand years' work across many worlds in the blink of an eye. You, like others before you, have the power to work outside of time."

Deiji suddenly felt very, very tired. She wanted to see this thing, this Hourglass.

"Mowat himself looked after many worlds," Arill continued. "It was only after he came back to his home world for Jayna that he really became involved in the affairs of Nigh. He has a great kinship with the sea, and he couldn't bear to see everyone at the mercy of the Balla. That's when he came up with the idea of the Code..."

"I see it!" She pointed one slender finger at the object that was rushing towards them, a large hourglass. Its frame was of a common brown wood, and it was half filled with a very fine white sand. It lay on its side so that no sand passed between the glass bulbs.

"Well," Arill prompted, "go on."

"Do I just… set it upright?" She wasn't sure.

"Yes, do it."

Deiji frowned as she approached it. She was positive it had to be much more complicated than this. She reached out and tipped it upright, though her fingers never seemed to actually touch it, and the sand continued to trickle once more.

"Is that it?"

"Yes. Let's get back to the others now – you'll want to stop Docin from causing any further problems."

She glanced at the scales that stood beyond and called them to her, setting them beside the Hourglass. The scales' trays were too full of Emeralds on one side, and she plucked them away, one by one, until they hung equally. She smiled and slipped the jewels into her pocket.

"For Zechi," she explained. "Maybe things will start going a little more smoothly for us. Now, let's go get Mowat."

וֹ

THE KING

"Arrrrgh!" Farlane's voice was high as he spilled his hot tea down his front.

Mangiat collided with Docin, barely missing him with the point of his blade as he fell. He wrestled

157

his arms around the man and glanced back to Deiji and had to smile – she was gone.

He released his hold on the Dragon Keeper, who stood and brushed himself off. He pointed his knife at him. "Stay where you are."

Geo and River clambered to their feet and walked over quizzically.

"Geo," Mangiat called out, without taking his eyes away from Docin, "he tried to harm Deiji!"

Docin paled, if possible, and Geo let out a snarl so fierce that the sailors awakened, hollering of an attack.

"Traitor!" Mangiat shouted brazenly.

The Pirates gathered round, their interest piqued at the notion of a traitorous man, and Zechi watched without comment from the tree line, his arms crossed. The boy, usually quick to jump to the defense of others in light of an unjust action, now had nothing to say.

Geo marched with angry strides, hot smoke wafting from his nostrils. Docin stumbled backwards and fell, dragging himself through the dirt.

"Ri... River?"

The blue Dragon stuck her spiked head into his face and let out a low, steady growl.

"STOP!"

Everyone looked to the sky, and Mangiat's heart soared.

There she was, descending from the heavens wearing the bright white sari she wore when she was in her realm. Her newly green eyes were bright and he was proud of her beauty.

"Enough! Leave Docin be," she commanded as she floated like a feather down to the ground. "It is time for us to move out. Sailors, back to your boats! Kindly leave my island. We will meet on the shore to discuss your ship and the movement of treasure."

The Captain nodded curtly to his men, and they obeyed, scurrying about, gathering their supplies and belongings before fading into the trees.

"Puff Puff, take our things and escort Zechi to the shore and wait with him there. I will call for you shortly. Zechi, take these." She opened her hand into his and Mangiat could see a stream of Emeralds sparkling into the boy's palm.

"Geo?" She turned to her friend.

The Dragon was sitting up, straight and dignified and ready for instruction. Mangiat noted how Deiji's voice seemed strangled when she spoke.

"Geo... Geo, I want you to go with Zechi. Protect him."

Geo nodded eagerly, not quite catching on. He turned to follow the others, glancing over his shoulder at River, who had stopped. He cocked his head to the side inquisitively.

Mangiat sighed and dropped his head. He knew what it was to be separated from one's beloved. He tried not to see the Dragon's pain when River stood as still as a statue beside her master, her sorrow hidden, her expression dutiful. Geo looked crushed. He looked helplessly to his friend, the girl.

Mangiat decided to speak up in Jai's place. "Even though she stood against Docin, Geo, she must now stand beside her master, even if she disagrees with his actions. You know and understand a Dragon's loyalties. She will stay."

Geo looked at Deiji and nodded. Defeated, he exchanged a glance with River one last time before continuing on with Zechi at his side.

Deiji turned to him. "We should go." They both looked to the white haired man, still sprawled across the dirt beside his beautiful Dragon. "Get off my Island, Docin." Her tone softened. "Thank you, River. Geo will be waiting for you."

They ran into the foliage.

₪

"Come on!" Deiji cried, throwing herself onto Mangiat's strong back. He galloped along the overgrown trails as quickly as he could muster, and prayed she had a plan.

"Follow this path to the left!" she shouted in his ear. They ran up a small knoll and out onto a deserted beach. He pulled his muscular body to a stop, barely missing the sharp cliff face that rose up from the beach without warning.

"Puff! I need you now!" The cat appeared without missing a beat.

"Yes, my Master?"

"Carry us to the cave!"

Puff Puff spread herself flat, into layers of cloud that could carry their weight. "Climb aboard, please," she squeaked. They stepped onto the platform hurriedly and it rose quicker than any Dragon could. Mangiat closed his eyes as the wind rushed by and the ground became a distant memory.

"We're here!" Deiji cried breathlessly, and Mangiat looked around.

"This is your home?" He was impressed.

It was a hole in the cliff that served as the door, with silken banners across the smaller holes that he understood to be windows. They went inside and he saw several rooms here, but he could not see where they led to, though he strained to look around.

He smiled at the jade Dragon that stood against the entrance, and he could see chairs and tables made of stone, covered in soft moss.

"This is what we're here for," she muttered, pushing past him. She knelt below a shelf that housed her many books and used her knife to pick the lock on a little leathern trunk. She tore the lock off and cast it aside, flipping back the lid.

Inside Mangiat saw a small pile of letters. He recognized his own seal and tidy scrawl, and he stared at her, amazed.

"You kept them?"

"Of course I did." She smiled. "But that's not what we're here for. *This* is what we want." She held up a tiny jar between her thumb and forefinger. He peered at it and could see a miniature, delicate squid floating inside it, slightly magnified through the water.

"What is it?"

"A Balla Seed."

"Come again?"

She snatched *The Keeper's Magic* off the shelf and flipped it open to page 784. She read aloud, *"One needs only to break the glass and drop the*

Seed into water to bring about a life-sized version of the creature, which will be eight times deadlier than the norm. One must also be sure the water they release it in is of volume enough to hold such a leviathan..."

"There are all sorts of vials." She motioned to the rest of the chest's contents, and indeed, it appeared that it contained several dozen similar items.

"Are they all different?"

"Yes, quite. I've looked at each and every one of them. Carefully, of course, because they're very fragile."

He hesitated frowning at the book. "Deiji, this sounds like very questionable magic."

"I know." Her expression was grave. "I read about every one of them in the book. There were some missing," she admitted, "but this could help us."

"How?"

"If I drop this little guy into the ocean, he will instantly grow into a full-grown Balla. The Mermaid's mortal enemy."

He grinned. "Good plan."

"Right. Let's meet the others."

ℷ

He could see the Pirates huddled around and talking amongst each other. Zechi and Geo were waiting on the beach nearby. Some of the sailors were making ready the lifeboats while others shifted from foot to foot uneasily, looking out over the water.

Deiji groaned. "They know their ship is missing."

"We'll think of something," he said confidently as they walked out onto the sandy beach. "Do you, er, have a plan?"

Deiji quickened her step and raised her voice. "My friends, there was an... incident concerning *The Lantern* yesterday. I'm sorry to say that it was capsized."

Captain Farlane turned a deep shade of purple. His men exchanged horrified glances, before looking back to Deiji in anger.

"I will fix this, I promise," she said, her voice wavering. He knew in his memory that she was not one to speak before crowds. The men began to stir with a restless anger, and shouts rang out above the roar of the surf. The girl could hardly stutter for words, and she began to back away.

Mangiat raised his hands defensively in front of him. "Now then, men, something can be done, it is sure," he declared loudly, but the men were not appeased. They had just began to shout even more angrily, when a squeaky, high voice rose above the crowd.

"You're going about this all the wrong way, of course."

All fell silent and stared up at the puffy little kitten, who sat nearby on her floating piece of cloud, licking her tiny paw and washing her face contentedly.

"What do you suggest we do?" Mangiat asked. Everyone was silent, listening intently for her reply.

"Well, you are all very amusing of course, and your simple bickering is quite charming, but wouldn't it be easier if I just put your ship back together?" She looked up and stared at them all, her blue eyes wide and waiting.

"Well, yes," Deiji said eagerly. "Would you?"

"Undoubtedly!" She let out a little laugh that was more of a squeak. "I can even save your crew."

"Then do it," Deiji commanded, and Mangiat was relieved.

"You are all *so* silly," she insisted. She floated out into the distance. They waited, holding their breath as they looked upon the still waters, the minutes passing slowly. The sun reflected off the surface sharply, and everyone squinted and held their hands over their eyes.

Suddenly, a great wave of water rose from the clear ocean surface. The bow of a ship beached, seemingly heading for the sky. Once it was nearly out of the water, it righted itself, and a large break down its middle melted together, as good as new.

There was a streak of cloud out to the horizon and the Puff disappeared, returning in seconds with a piece of driftwood, a famished sailor clinging to it. She placed it on the resurrected ship and flew off, again and again, each time returning with another member of the crew.

When they each got to their feet and waved to their comrades on the shore, their health restored, the men cheered and laughed, clambering into the lifeboats happily. Captain Farlane walked up to Deiji.

"Thank you," he said simply. The girl smiled, and they bowed to one another.

"The treasure is in your hold," Deiji said, waving her palm over the ship that sat in the distance.

"You have kept your word, after all this." Farlane was impressed.

"I always do."

"Where are you headed now?" the Captain inquired.

"Treehorn Island."

"Would you like to take passage on our ship?" he offered.

Mangiat leaned in on the conversation. "Yes. Yes, we would be much obliged, my good sir."

The Captain nodded thoughtfully. "These Mermaids and the problem you were discussing with Docin... If there were something we could do..."

"Yes?"

"I believe we may be of some help in locating your kidnapped friend."

"Really?" His eyes widened in excitement. "How is this?"

The Captain smiled. "If Dragons are our mythical enemies, then Mermaids are our friends."

Chapter Ten
Treehorn Island

THE KEEPER OF FIRE

" *Well*, it looks as though you won't be avoiding the forecastle this time!" Deiji said with a hearty laugh. She felt almost giddy as she watched the Centaur stare into the doorway apprehensively, clutching his things close to his body.

They were underway. The crew was working the ship with Puff's assistance for speed as Deiji, Mangiat and Zechi got settled in. Micid was keeping herself busied and always at a distance from the freed visitors.

Deiji walked out onto the deck, breathing the fresh sea air with satisfaction. She glanced up at Geo who had taken his place among the ratlines, looking back at the Island with apparent longing.

"You'll be together soon," she called up to her best friend with assurance. "I will see to it." She walked along, somewhat upset, though slightly cheered at the affections of her Dragon.

Arill was dashing frantically in the water beside them, trying to keep up, using the ship's wake as a boost. She smiled down over the railing. Arill had been such a help throughout this ordeal… His knowledge was so valuable. She looked to the bright open sky.

There were others who could offer her council in such times. There were others who carried the wisdom of the world and the stars. The beginnings of a plan began to form within her mind and she met Mangiat as he followed her onto the deck. "Mangiat."

He smiled. She loved that smile, so sincere and free. "Mangiat, we have one more stop to make."

"And where is that?" He looked slightly apprehensive when she didn't answer. She knew he felt himself dragged about mercilessly. He was such a creature by design to be expectant that each day should unfold as the one before it. He was a creature of the trees.

She closed her eyes and they both lifted off the boat and into the sky. She opened her eyes when Mangiat started shouting in surprise. She began to laugh as they flew into the clouds freely, and she grabbed him by the wrist.

They passed through the thinnest of clouds. When they moved through the thicker ones, they were blasted by a blanket of dampness. They rose through a gap in the thickest cloud floor and came to rest upon it.

Mangiat began to stamp his hooves in earnest, scared to death of the flimsy, misty flooring that shifted beneath them.

Deiji cocked an eyebrow at him. "You have not been here? When you were a student under Mowat, where did he train you?"

"The woods," he groaned. "On the *ground.*"

She laughed. "Do not worry so! I spent some time here when I was trained."

The clouds spread put for miles before them, blindingly white and textured as any landscape. It was quiet and still, for no breezes blew here, and the silence was absolute. There were slight patches of thin cloud, and holes even, so that the land was visible, far, far below.

Mangiat shuddered. "What are we doing here?" He used his forearm to wipe an anxious sweat from his rigid brow.

"We're here to see a friend."

"*... People of the wind, O!*" The voice was faint, coming across the vast expanse of whiteness.

Mangiat looked stunned, alert and afraid. "What was that?" he asked quickly, alarmed.

It was a single voice, and Deiji recognized it as Weyes's, and he was singing to his brothers.

"It is one of the Sties. The People of the Wind."

"I have heard you speak of them before."

"They watch over the affairs of the Nigh world and offer insight to those like myself."

"I understand." He still looked unconvinced.

"We should find him." They began to walk along the clouds, somewhat unsteadily, for Mangiat's four legs wobbled with uncertain steps, and she delayed, waiting.

"Let us try leaping, shall we?" she suggested without impatience, and she sprang off the clouds and high into the air, falling slowly... So slowly that when she lost her balance and landed on her back, she laughed, for no harm had come to her.

Mangiat followed her movements with a grin, and the two flew into the air, descending slowly before rising again. They bounded east across the clouds together in the direction of the voice.

They laughed, a happy pair as they crossed rhythms above the endless stretch of cloud. Their laughter was the only other sound beside the Stie, for it was eerily quiet here. Deiji flew high as Mangiat landed below, and he rose as she landed and they laughed for joy. They came to a stop when they heard the loud chanting of the single Stie.

"Puff is from here, you know," she panted as they walked the rest of the way.

*"My soul sings praises of the world
above, below.
It is greater than that of all the Earth,
above, below.
Above, below, I sit here between all
That falls to and fro.
My soul..."*

Weyes. He reminded her of a great spirit, nearly transparent, his short hair and the edges of his clothing flapping freely, as if caught by a continual flow of wind. He looked a colorless Man, though he held a certain ethereal dignity about him that he couldn't have ever been so common a creature.

This being sat on a piece of cloud, meditating before his tea. He did not seem to acknowledge their presence at first, then finally gave a wave of his hand and two more porcelain cups appeared. Deiji gave Mangiat an encouraging smile as she accepted her steaming cup graciously, with both hands.

Weyes finished his chanting and looked upon his visitors. "Deiji." His voice was calm, quiet. "It has been a short while." It had been five years.

"Yes, my friend." Deiji bowed in a manner of respect. "I have come to you for counsel. Where are your brothers?" She glanced around almost expectantly.

His answer was simple. "Elsewhere."

"Ah."

"We meet once every hundred years if we must. I dare say last time was too soon." He stared openly at Mangiat.

"Oh!" Deiji cried, catching herself. "This is Mangiat. He is helping me on my quest, and he is... He is to be my spouse." Her ears burned at the words, but she said them proudly.

"That is well," Weyes nodded in thoughtful approval. "Now, what is the purpose you have sought me for counsel?" She understood that he was already prepared to bid them farewell.

Deiji waved her hand over a bit of cloud beside her, which shaped itself into a deep chair and she sank into it. She glanced at Mangiat who held up a single hand in decline. She drank from her cup before speaking.

"We are here to gain insight on the current state of things in and around Nigh," she began slowly, "as Mowat has been kidnapped."

"I see." Weyes nodded quietly. "I have seen this. And it is in your mind to find him?"

"And to rescue him," she added pointedly.

"Ah, yes, there is that." He mused on this a while, refilling his tea by wringing out a bit of cloud.

Deiji leaned forward. "Do you know if he is alive? I mean, is he all right?"

"Let us see to your friend. Let us see the day he disappeared," he said sagely, and he whisked his palm across the cloud before them, and a hole appeared in its center.

The image of the dark, angry sea of the Southern Ocean came clear, and they could see a small rowboat, miniscule beside the powerful waves around it. The memory drew in closer, and both Deiji and Mangiat leaned forward. Lightning flashed and thunder growled in the distance.

Mowat's face was tired but earnest as the waters thrashed him about. His white beard and hair were plastered to his face and he was soaked to the bone. He rowed quickly, though the waves tossed him about carelessly and he had no power over the vessel.

Deiji was struck by an incredible realization – Mowat was frightened.

A large wave rose with the rush of a violent wind, and one of his oars broke. The man scrambled for the pieces, but they were gone. He dropped into the belly of the boat, clinging to the wooden seat, fighting no longer.

"Jai…" His voice was scarcely a whimper. Another wave rose and his boat capsized. It floated there, facedown for a time, wandering aimlessly across the stormy waters.

"Mowat?" Deiji asked the void. He never surfaced. "Weyes, where did he go?" she demanded, and as she spoke she saw the brief splash of three Mermaid tails as they dove under, illuminated by the flashing lightning.

She looked up at the Stie, who buried the vision underneath the clouds.

"So it *was* the Merpeople," she affirmed.

"Indeed. I believe it is a trap."

"A trap?" She had not thought of this. "I knew the Merpeople wanted the Rune, but I did not know they were informed as to whose possession it was in."

"They have had him in their hands for several days now. He could have told them anything, if desperate. And they knew you would come for him."

"And I will. It is my life for Mowat's," she said proudly.

"Not the wisest of decisions," Weyes rebuked her gently.

"How so?" It was almost a challenge.

"If it is indeed a trap," Weyes said carefully, "then you are risking something greater than your own life."

"And that is?" Mangiat spoke suddenly, forcefully, having remained silent all this time. Deiji could see the pain and concern in his dark eyes.

Weyes waited for the small outburst to pass, and he spoke on. "The Rune," he said mildly, and she heard a whisper of his next thoughts in the wind. *"Naturally."*

They fell silent to pondering with the fullness of this thought. The Stie gestured at her necklace, where the stone now sat snugly. "Once they have the Rune they will take part in an ancient ritual that has never been fulfilled. They will flood the Earth and make it their own."

Finally, Deiji spoke, screwing up her face pensively. "Flood the Earth? You are right, if that is even possible. The Rune is most valuable. If we can preempt such an attempt to steal it, and plan for it, then maybe we can work around this." Her eyes met Mangiat's and they exchanged a silent confirmation of such a plan.

"Where shall we start?" Mangiat asked her, but Weyes supplied the answer.

"Treehorn Island. But be wary, my friends. You can be within the waters, but on the Island's surface, no magic can be cast."

Deiji's eyes widened, her long lashes pulled all the way back. "No magic? You mean it is a Dead Rock?" Mangiat glanced at her with question.

"I have read of such places, only I did not dream they existed!"

"Guard the Rune, Jai," Weyes insisted. "The Rune of Life is yours to protect, and you would do well to save your friend without losing it to the Merpeople. There is, however, a more immediate threat at hand. Don't go looking for the Merpeople; the only way they will succeed is if they take the Rune from you."

"Threat? What threat?" She asked, ignoring his last statement.

Once again Weyes swept his hand across the sky below their feet and they looked down into the world. They hovered over the Deep Forest, and the scene that unfolded before them left both speechless.

ןּ

GENERAL MORIM

"Mark that one. And that one over there!"

"Bring the horses around!"

General Morim walked along the stream on the edge of the Deep Forest, watching the men noisily begin their work of their trade with their axes. They were hacking away at trees and shouting at one another. Logs lay strewn about the site, waiting for the horses to haul them away. He sighed.

He felt some guilt at the issue, but he also believed it was necessary. Already they had lost a man, a blacksmith who must now share his shops with an Elf. He opted for this new trade offered and was crushed by a falling tree on his second day. There was a lot to learn in this business.

"What do you think, Sire?" Gance's voice startled him as the man took his place at his side.

Morim nervously fingered the scepter he had grown so accustomed to.

"I think that so long as we stick to our set quota – one acre per week – then there may be less anger from the Mystical peoples."

"What the Mystical creatures do, or threaten to do is of no concern," Gance retorted. "Bowen and many of his men have gone to Treehorn Island to claim the jewels from Par Jaque's new camp, my king. Money is power, and all will bow to you for it!"

"They have gone again?" Morim asked in earnest, for he did not like the notion of Elvin slavery, and couldn't imagine that Gance, being an Elf, did either.

"Yes, yes," Gance waved one hand passively. "And he will go again and again until you are the wealthiest king in all the histories of Nigh. And since we have done as Bowen requested with the increase of production here, he now offers two hundred rebel men to guard and enforce our efforts here, as well as promote the permanent sanction for the separation of Man and Mystical!"

General Morim felt an old familiar discomfort at this. After all that King Mangiat and his friends had done to unite the world, it seemed too simple, too easy, perhaps, to tear it in two once more.

"Tell him, Nia." Gance interrupted, and he glanced warily at the frail woman who trailed behind him, unconvinced of such a show of vulnerability.

175

"You have indeed been the king we have waited for." Her words gushed forth as blood from a severed limb, and he winced.

She touched her withered hand to his arm. "This is meant to be, my king. Man is more deserved than his neighboring brethren, and it is time to take back what is ours."

"We shall drive them from your villages, your schools and stations of trade!" The Elf pumped his bony fist into the air. "It is time that our people withdraw from yours and return to the life we've known for two hundred years and more."

₪

THE KEEPER OF FIRE

She looked at Mangiat, whose face was reddened in such a fit of anger she had never seen. He sputtered and made for speech, but could not. Deiji, however, spoke with assuredness.

"What do we do, Weyes? How can we prevent such a pending separation?"

The Stie kept his gaze on the true King of Nigh and did not answer at first, then said in a low voice, "they are not meant to live together, Man and Mystical. The world is still not one."

"Then you agree they are to be separated?" she asked, astonished.

"Not this way. Another way, perhaps, but not this way." He stared intently into his teacup.

"How *dare* they!" Mangiat finally found his voice, and he began to scream of treachery and loyalties until he shouted himself into silence, his eyes closed in some private sorrow.

"What shall we do?" Deiji asked softly, taking the hand of her beloved, her eyes closing with his in harmony.

The Stie was clear. "I think you know."

"Then they must go back." She sighed heavily.

"Back? Back where?" Mangiat's eyes opened abruptly and he stared at her. "Who must go back?"

"Man. It is time they go back to the water."

₪

THE KING

They rejoined the crew, and Mangiat listened intently as Deiji slyly told him she had let an entire day and a half pass them by, so that the ship was already as far north as the Pirate's Islands. They had already passed by Pegasus Point. He would not have to endure the sea much longer.

He looked at his love thankfully, but could scarcely force a laugh. The kingdom – his kingdom – was being divided and ravaged while he sat a hundred and more miles away. His dearest confidant and general had defied his orders and betrayed him to the Nigh Elders, the scribes... And even if Man consented to go back to the waters, what then? Nigh would still need a king.

He could see Zechi on the deck in a fresh change of clothes. Polk was perched on his shoulder as they stared out to the grey sea.

"Zechi."

"Hello!" He seemed cheered at the fresh air and adventure, but Mangiat had no heart for games and laughter. He peered closer and found the boy pale.

"You are young and in good health, my friend. Why do you seem ill?"

"I have difficulty living apart from the trees, is all," he admitted. "I am fine, do not worry yourself."

"I understand completely." Mangiat actually smiled. Here was this boy, nay, a man after his own heart!

Zechi looked into his face and they found the same joke. "So where have you been?" He grinned.

"Jai and myself had matters to attend to."

"Ah, that is what we figured," Zechi said with a smile as he urged Polk to take flight again. They watched the falcon soar into the air and circle the main mast.

"I hope you were not worried."

Zechi laughed. "Oh, no. You were with Jai," he said matter-of-factly. "Did you find anything new concerning Mowat?"

Mangiat looked away and he knew he must tell the boy everything. He quickly explained Morim's doings, and watched as the boy's green eyes sparked with rage.

"They will not get away with this!" Zechi cried, and Mangiat nodded in agreement.

He looked over the rail at the familiar sight of the Dolphin leaping through the waters, and he stared out at the distant marshland they passed by. Then the Captain shouted, "Land ho! Treehorn Island!"

"Land ho!" his men chorused in agreement. Deiji sidled up next to him after a while and slipped her arm through his. He rested his head against hers for a moment, and they listened to the crew scurry around, making preparations. Finally, she spoke.

"I have spoken to the Captain. By dawn we will leave the ship and take Treehorn Island."

"Thank you." He continued to stare at the horizon. Would they find Mowat here? He sighed at the ache he found was not in his head, but in his heart.

₪

His four knees were quite stiff when they next glimpsed the Island through the early morning's fog. It was a dreary place, he decided.

The fog sat heavy and thick upon the water, the sky blotted out by the gray mist. Rotted seaweed bobbed about everywhere aimlessly, and it stank as it bumped into the passing ship and clung there, like a parasite. The chill here brought a damp clamminess to him, and he felt as though it would never leave his bones.

"Just as I remember it," Deiji said darkly, and Mangiat wished she hadn't, for it only heightened the mood of the place.

Ruan called down from the crow's nest, "land ho! Hard t' starboard!" Out of the fog rose a mass of land so suddenly that Mangiat feared they would crash upon it. But the men were true to their trade, and the ship slowed easily.

The sailors began their preparation for disembarking, when suddenly Puff's voice rang out, loud and astonished, "Master, I cannot go any further!" All eyes fell upon the little cat, who seemed to be fighting against an invisible wall. She could not venture onto the side of the ship nearest to the Island.

Deiji groaned. "I was afraid of this."

"What is it?" Zechi asked, and Mangiat made to answer, but the Pirates launched into a series of superstitious explanations.

"It is ghosts! Spirits from the underworld."

"The slave drivers! They keep immortals from disturbing their cause!"

"It is the Elves themselves – they despise any magic deeper than theirs."

Deiji cut in, loudly and lordly, "it is a place devoid of magic, lad. It is called a Dead Rock. No magical influence can be had here."

One by one each person looked at the girl with question. She finally cried out impatiently, "all right! All right! Yes, it means I am nothing but a human there."

"Then you are not going," Mangiat said firmly.

"Excuse me?" All eyes shot from the girl and back to himself with apparent amusement and interest.

"If you take one step onto that Island you will become quite vulnerable. We can't risk anything untoward – "

"I can take care of myself," she said coldly.

"I tell you, we cannot risk it!"

"Excuse me," Zechi waved his hand a bit and stepped between them. "May I speak? Yes?" They glared at him, but he pressed on. "Okay, so if I am informed correctly, Deiji will be needed underwater to deal with the Merpeople in the search for Mowat, correct?"

"But Mowat could be *on* the Island. We don't know for sure," Deiji protested, but Zechi would have none of it.

"Last time you came here as a Mermaid, you were under water and the magic remained intact, correct?"

She nodded.

"Then we will handle Treehorn Island. You need to cover the island's base."

"Who is 'we?'" Mangiat asked skeptically.

"The Pirates, Geo and myself." The boy laughed, though he spoke with authority and pride. A thought began to worm its way into Mangiat's mind and take form there.

"And what of myself?" he asked with a small smile – what it was to be king and take an order from one's student!

Deiji was the one to laugh this time. "I am sure Puff Puff can come up with something."

ɲ

THE BOY

"Onward, men!" Captain Farlane's voice rang out as the Pirates rushed up the beach. Zechi's expression was firm. This was his moment, his meaning.

The ground ahead of them became rocky as they made their way up, and the rotten foliage was thick. Zechi pressed his hand against the base of a withered tree, waiting for the familiar warmth that came through its trunk and to his fingertips, but there was nothing. He felt strangely cut off. The tree usually responded, not in words, but with a listening ear and a strong soul. These trees were... *dead*.

There was a smell here on this island, and it was smell of dead things that remain unburied. There was too much fog here, he thought quickly, breathing lightly. He stepped away from the tree and saw the men scrambling over the rise, then hastily followed them.

Once over the top, he could see most of the Island before him. There was another ridge blocking his view to the far side. He figured he should start there. A stagnant river that ran into the ocean split Treehorn Island into three sections, and it was in this river that Zechi saw the splash of a colorful orange tailfin.

"Look!" he pointed, and all the men stared. Farlane stepped forward. "We must ask her what she is doing here – where Mowat is!"

"I will deal with this," the Captain said briskly, and he knelt by the water. Sure enough, a black-haired Mermaid lifted her head to his, and they touched and spoke. What was said Zechi could not hear, as they met within their own minds, but it was not long before he had his answers.

"Your friend is on the Island!" Farlane called out, his smile wide beneath his beard as he stood.

Zechi cheered. "We need to tell Deiji…" He looked at the group of men, but Micid stepped forward.

"I will tell them." And before he could protest, she had waddled back down to the beach.

Zechi did not trust the woman, but his focus must be on Mowat. If he was truly on this island, it was imperative he be found, and soon, before another tangent overtook their attention.

"How did you get her to tell you the truth?"

The Captain grinned. "It was simple. She asked if I was here to rescue a man, and I said no, but I was to deliver a shipment to the mines. Apparently there's a dock on the far side of the Island," he added brightly. "She seemed disappointed, and it was quite obvious that she waits to fight Mowat's savior. Such things they did not teach at the Nigh Academy!"

Zechi stared at him. "One day you will have to tell me about yourself."

Farlane smiled serenely. "Ah, lad, such a day may never come."

He grinned back at the Captain, pleased with the man's mystery. "Let's go!"

They jogged up the second steep incline, hurrying, unsure of what might be seen. Zechi dug his leather boots into the loose rock, slipping a little, and they came to the crest of the hill. Geo stood at his side and they all gazed downward, speechless.

It was a quarry. Dozens of Elves stood in shackles and chains as they hauled rocks and water.

It was exceedingly hard labor, and he could see how they strained against their loads. They mined for the Rubies, Sapphires and other such jewels as flowed through Nigh.

Some wept and looked haggard, as though they had gone days without sleep, but most were mute. They were streaked with dirt, their tattered clothes showing their nakedness and the sharpness of their ribs, as they starved.

Zechi looked over at the Captain sharply. "What is this?" he demanded.

"This is the shame of Nigh. The Elves mine the jewels, which are shipped into the great city itself for an incredible sum. This travesty is not spoken of within the courts of Nigh. It is one of many things of this sort that incited the Pirates' ancestors to leave the villages of Man. And myself," he added.

Zechi felt angry. What other things had Man done that had gone so unnoticed as this? Why had he not heard of this, though he spent five years in the Nigh court? He looked out at the three rivers that divided the Island and knew he must move quickly.

"Free them." He uttered these words with strength. Geo nodded in full agreement.

"Pardon?"

He looked at Farlane. "Free the Elves. Put an end to this." The man paused to ponder this, but nodded.

"Sir!" the red-haired Ruan called out. "There are Men, sir!"

"Hide!" Captain Farlane hissed, and they all ducked low into the brush, even Geo, who caused his flesh to turn the color of the grass around him.

184

They could see a man down in the quarry, and this man led a dozen soldiers into the campground. An animated conversation between this man and one of the overseers took place below them, and Zechi squinted, then realized...

"I know him... It is Bowen! And that man is Par Jaque!"

Deiji was not going to be happy to hear about this.

The Pirate beside him grunted, and Zechi suddenly felt uncomfortable as he watched one of Bowen's soldiers thrust an Elf bound in rope down at Par Jaque's feet in exchange for several large satchels that he knew to be packed with jewels. They could hear snippets of conversation floating up to where they hid.

"It's an awful business, it is," Bowen muttered as the Elf was taken away.

Par Jaque nodded. "It is the only reliable trade I have yet found that produces enough money to establish myself. Since my wife left me I have been struggling to build up my coffers and make myself worthy of her once more. I want her to have no excuse not to come home."

The two men wandered into the quarry dugout together and disappeared.

Zechi frowned. Maia left her husband? Deiji was going to want to know this!

He looked over at the Captain once more. "Free them all," he commanded. "I am going to look for Mowat."

ת

THE KING

"Did you see anything?" Mangiat called down to Deiji as she and Arill resurfaced from the depths of the sea.

She shook her head angrily at him. "There is nothing down there. I am afraid Treehorn Island is not the place. We have wasted two hours!"

Arill began to chatter excitedly next to her, and once again Mangiat wished for the moment that he could join in. But with this longing came the fear, which bubbled up and rose to his throat so suddenly he almost vomited. His sweat stood out cold on his body.

"That's it!" Deiji cried in reply.

"What?" He was irritated, impatient as he bent over the ship's railing.

She grinned. "We're at the wrong place. There are no Merpeople here. They're at the Mermaid fortress. In Whale Waters. They must be! Where else would they gather in anticipation of such a ceremony?"

He groaned. "That is clear on the other side of the *world!* Are we to spend days at sea after all this?" His head drooped to his chest, defeated.

"I have an idea."

He lifted his head to see Jai raise her arms and a ring of blue light coned out towards the sky. She floated up aside Arill, and rose out of the water. Mangiat's hooves lifted from the deck and he started. A strange silver glow emanated from his

186

friends, and he glanced at his own arms, surprised that his body carried the same shine.

The three lifted up high into the clouds and the ocean rushed by below. Soon they passed over the Deep Forest – too fast to see anything of their world – and then over Mount Odel and down to the Nigh court… They flew over the sea once more, then into the ocean, past the Trinity Islands, down to where the Mermaid Fortress lay.

רּ

Mangiat treaded the warm water nervously, one hand resting on Arill's dorsal fin for support. He knew the Dolphin would not let him drown, but it did not make this any easier. He looked at Deiji, who was already in Mermaid form.

"Are you ready?" she asked him with an encouraging smile.

"As ready as possible." He tried not to whimper. He took a deep breath and thought about what lay ahead. It wasn't a bad place, the sea, not really… It was just water, lots of water, and mysterious creatures that could approach one from any unsuspecting angle; not just from behind, but above and below... He shook these thoughts from his worried mind, but he must have shaken his body as well, for Deiji looked at him with concern.

"Are you okay?"

"Yes. Yes, I am." He took another deep breath, dreading his farewell to the tropical sun that filled these shallow reef waters with light, such a contrast to Treehorn Island.

"Puff!" the girl called to her cat.

"Yes?" Puff floated down lazily and rested on a bit of cloud right above the surface of the water, bobbing around in accordance to the movements of the waves.

"Join with Mangiat. Make him a Merman. Blue tail. Do as he says and stay with him until he releases you, even if I ask you to do otherwise."

This last comment made him uneasy, but he was caught up in this new thing, and it was the cat joining herself to him. It was odd, he thought, as he felt his four limbs join together into one. His black horse's body turned a deep blue and scales grew rapidly where fur was. His upper body remained the same, and this was a comfort to him. He lost his hooves and gained fins of sheer silver, and found himself floundering around helplessly.

When his head went underwater he panicked, convinced he would suffocate, then he realized he could breathe. He looked around at the two spectators who laughed. He tried to right himself, but was only twisting around in the water.

"My, you certainly seem coordinated," Arill teased. "Deiji always described you as a graceful creature." It was a marvel to Mangiat that he could understand this Dolphin whom he had heard so much about but had never spoken to.

"Leave him be," Deiji smiled, and he recognized the grace and simple beauty of her Mermaid form, which she so easily carried into her own. She splashed about in delight beside Arill, clearly pleased. The stone on her sword blazed a dozen brilliant colors.

Mangiat tried to move his long tail four different ways at once as he was used to, but the result was an odd jerking movement that left him floundering.

"Move your tail up and down like this, with your body flat in the water, your tail behind you," Arill offered, and he and Deiji demonstrated, swimming in circles around him until he was dizzy. Nevertheless, their advice was true to his new form, and he was soon able to mimic them until they all swam in a circle together. Arill leapt out of the water for joy, and his return sent a froth of bubbles that tickled Mangiat's face and made him laugh.

"I've got it!" he said proudly. "I really do." And he broke form and began to swim about in every which way, down and back up to the surface and all around.

"Wonderful." Deiji smiled at him faintly, as if reliving some distant memory. "Ready?"

"Absolutely."

The three turned tail to sky and dove into the depths. The water was warm, blue and pristine, the sun shimmering off the reef and all across the sand. Silver fish flitted in and out of the reef, and he found himself hungry for them, surprisingly happy to be in the sea.

They could see the Mermaid Fortress far below, but not a soul was in sight. The underwater castle was made of stone, and its turrets were tall and joined each hall to the main building. A great court stood in the center, a pillared altar erected on the far wall.

"There have definitely been Merpeople here!" Deiji cried. "Last time I saw this place, it was covered in algae and the stone was cracked!"

The court was alight with more colorful fish, and he began to feel drawn to them again. Jai started to call out the song of the Mermaid. Mangiat laughed, drawn to the sound of it. He suddenly wanted to hug her, wrap his tailfin around hers...

"Mermaids are extremely social creatures," she explained, breaking him out of his longings. "If there are other Merpeople about, they will be compelled to respond."

Arill too was letting out a soft melody of some sort, but he knew it was more for Mowat. They swam into the depths in this fashion with the Mermaid and the Dolphin calling out this way. Mangiat felt a slight sheepish, but he joined in.

"We must be quiet for a time," Arill warned, "one must leave an interval for them to respond to us."

Sure enough, the three fell silent and there came the distant echo of a warm song.

"There!" They swam as quickly as they could towards the sea floor, the great fortress growing ever nearer.

"Use caution!" Arill called. "The Merman responding sounds a little too inviting. It should be questioning us, not inviting us to come." They slowed their pace as they neared the spot. Indeed, the castle's court was clean and well manicured, though it was as still as a grave.

"Shall we spread out?" Arill asked, and Mangiat looked at the altar on the far side of the open court.

"I want to see that," he pointed to it. They approached the table cautiously and saw it was a ceremonial altar made of heavy stone. There were characters scrawled across it, and a hole in the center. He looked at the circular hole and thought of only one thing that could sit snugly inside it.

"Jai…"

He felt the vibrations before he saw the net. It flew through the water at them as they hovered over the stone altar, and stones that were tied to the edges of the ropes weighed them down when it struck.

"Oh no!"

A handful of Merpeople came pouring out from the castle halls, and they brandished spears.

"You were right," said a large, muscular Merman, not turning his gaze away from his captives. "She came."

₪

THE DRAGON KEEPER

High above the Deep Forest a man and his Dragon flew gently along the breezes. Docin patted River's scaly neck fondly. He rested his head upon her for a moment.

"Thank you for not abandoning me," he whispered, praying his light touch would relay his meaning to her. He knew she was bitter at him for his treatment toward their new friends. Angry at him for separating her from her new mate. There is not a sin a Man can commit greater than parting a

Dragon from her love. But, as a Dragon of old, she assuredly retained her Dragon loyalty. And yet he was still ashamed.

The Merpeople, ah, the Merpeople. What could he have done, than obey them? The need for the plant was a ruse, a lie for an excuse to be on the mainland. He knew the Merpeople planned to flood the Earth so that none could ever take the ocean from them again. Only the mountain ranges of Nigh would remain uncovered. In exchange for the Rune these would be his to preserve as a Dragon haven, for he loved his Dragons, as if they were his very children.

The Dragons with their magic would keep him young. Here he was, centuries old, and he hardly looked thirty! His conscience plagued him at times, but he knew grimly that it was necessary.

They swooped down low over the hills and his light eyes widened in surprise at the sight that spread out below them. "There was never a clearing here," Docin muttered.

There were tents set up in a semicircle on the far end of the campsite, and men bustled about here and there, cooking and washing clothes in the stream. On the opposite end tree stumps studded the area, and Docin was surprised. He had never heard of a thing as this. They were taking trees! And for what?

People lived in earthen huts, strengthened by thatch, straw… Buildings of stone, maybe. They never had need for more wood than one could gather off the ground.

But he could see it plainly before him. There were men who drove horses that hauled the logs out of the camp, and men who cut the wood where it fell to carry out in carts drawn by mules.

"Let us spy on this new thing!" Docin called down, and River dropped her left wing and they fell to the Earth.

Chapter Eleven
Mowat

THE BOY

The fight was furious. And magicless. Captain Farlane and his men raced down into the quarry and attacked with swords and daggers while the overseers fought back with their whips. But these slave drivers were nowhere near as intimidating as Par Jaque with his handful of trained soldiers, who held their spears. These fought with the grace of men who offer their lives in battle for a purpose, and they fought the Pirates.

Many of the men fell into the rock and rubble. Zechi paused and watched as the Captain found himself sword to sword on a wooden beam above a tunnel support. He fought gallantly and Zechi had to push himself to keep moving. He was afraid for the men, but their battle bought him time, and he must hurry, lest their lives be waste. Even Polk was doing his part, screeching and diving into the crowd and tearing at soldier's eyes with his talons.

Geo was by far the more feared of any, for most who saw him ran. He dove again and again, blowing fire, baring his poisonous claws... They would win this because of him.

Zechi made his way along the rim of the quarry pit, his dagger drawn. He moved briskly, searching for a small cage or corner where Jai's Master might be kept. "Mowat?"

Then a weak, distant voice came from up above, through the sounds of fighting. "Help! Help me, please!"

Zechi turned at the sound and saw he faced a sheer rock wall. Another ridge. There were not many grooves for his fingers, and it was very high. It looked to be quite dangerous if he should try to climb it. He grinned.

He stepped forward and began to climb up quickly, finding every little edge with his fingertips, every slight foothold with assuredness.

"Oh no, you don't!" Someone snatched at his ankle from behind, and Zechi fell the short way to the ground, landed on his feet and spun around. It was the Miller Bowen in his new black clothes, fat now with overfeeding, long whip in hand. He flicked his whip and delivered quite a startling lash to Zechi's face.

Zechi drew a dagger from his boot and charged at the man. Bowen snarled and moved aside with heavy steps, his whip flapping about uselessly. He grabbed Zechi roughly around the neck with his free arm and threw him to the ground.

Choking, Zechi grunted as the gravel scuffed under his falling form. His elbow stung as he landed upon it, and he jumped back to his feet quickly, lunging at Bowen.

"Oh!" the man cried out in surprise as Zechi's blade stuck into his vitals. The boy stood back silently as Bowen fell back into the rubble. He did not retrieve his knife. "Help me, please!" Bowen gasped in shock.

Zechi frowned. "I've never..." He could not finish aloud. "*I have never killed,*" he said quietly in the privacy of his mind. He turned grimly towards the cliff face and began to climb away from the dying man. It was the first time he would take a life.

The handholds became scarce as he neared the top, and he slipped and nearly fell again. His feet scuffed against the sheer rock, and he wished for a moment that he had asked Geo to carry him...

Panting heavily, he pulled himself over the top and rolled onto the ridge. He drew himself to all fours and looked down the other side.

ℵ

THE KING

Jai was struggling against the nets, drawing her sword and hacking away as she cursed them. Mangiat closed his eyes. The joys of being a Merman were gone. There was nothing worse than to rest under the water's pressure and remain captive there.

"Be still!" the Merman yelled at them, and he drew one large hand across the net. Mangiat found he could not move at all, and it was a moment until the magic wore off completely.

Their captor held an enormous trident of silver. He had a very large and thick blue tail fin, and his short hair and beard were silver. A curved blue seashell hung about his neck, held by strings of seaweed. He had a deep scar that crossed both his lips, and when he sneered his teeth showed beneath his nose. Deiji was muttering something under her breath, her eyes closed, head bowed. The net vanished.

"*Ciechi!*" she cried to their captors, and a stream of heated rocks bubbled the water around them and struck the Merman in the chest. He cried out in pain and mumbled a spell to heal himself.

"Deiji, don't!" a whiny voice called out.

He looked up and saw a Mermaid, much younger than this male who had trapped them. Her tailfin was a faded purple, her skin very brown. Her hair was a light yellow, and it looked too yellow to be paired to such a dark shade of skin. He recognized her...

Mangiat glanced at Deiji and was surprised to see her staring, openmouthed, at this girl.

"Do we know her?" he asked.

Deiji stared on, stunned. "Elail?"

ℶ

He would never forget the way Deiji looked at her friend now. It was with a strong mixture of awe and disappointment. Mangiat was no longer scared, and he knew Arill was calm as well. Deiji would keep them from harm, he was certain. But he knew the conversation to follow would not be a pleasant one.

"Elail?" She still looked dumbstruck. The Mermaid suddenly looked ashamed.

"Elail… *Why?*" Deiji's voice was suddenly loud and overbearing. Angry.

Nearly a dozen Merpeople of all different colors were encircled around the three captives, and they winced at her voice. Mangiat smiled.

"It is not me, or my doing," Elail hastily explained, "It's…" Her voice trailed off and she motioned towards the large Merman who was preparing another net.

"And who are you, exactly?" Deiji demanded.

The Merman looked up. "I am Eligh," he answered coldly.

"Elail's father!" Deiji exclaimed. "It is so nice to meet – " She stopped in her speech and looked confused. And once again, her anger overcame her. "What is going on? Did I not save you before? Did I not defeat the Balla? Why do you do this?"

Elail looked sheepish. "I told everyone what you did, how you saved my family, only – "

"Only we need the Rune!" Eligh cut in.

"Getting right to the point, are we?" Mangiat cut in cheerfully.

"Give it to me now!" the Merman cried, ignoring him.

"Do not!" Arill snapped.

"Give me that sword! Or I shall take it from you!" Eligh motioned to the sword and the false stone that gave forth light and color in Arill's presence. He gave a signal of his hand and there was a flurry of movement as the Merpeople descended upon Deiji, and in the brief struggle, she lost the sword. The Merpeople crowded around it.

"How shall we take the stone out?"

"Pry it off! Here is my knife!"

"Do not break it!" Eligh said sternly. A knife was put to it and the stone was handed to a nearby Merman who swam away hurriedly. They watched him approach the altar and place the stone into the space that existed for it. They all sat back expectantly.

"To the eternal city!" Eligh cried, and the Merpeople cheered.

"Why do you want the Rune?" Deiji asked softly, and Mangiat too was intrigued.

"Immortality." The answer came easily.

"Come again?"

He smiled. "Tell them, my daughter." He turned back to Deiji's sword, which he was inspecting with a look of pleasure upon his face.

Elail blushed and looked down. "Yes, father."

Mangiat glared at her openly, and he was pleased when her speech faltered.

"It… It is for the Mermaid Fortress." Some excitement rekindled on her face as she explained, and it was obvious that she could not help it. "Do you remember when it was abandoned and all in disarray?"

"Absolutely."

"Well, it has been reborn! After all that you did for us, we began to live in larger numbers again. And we have rebuilt our court from the ruins."

"That is wonderful!"

"There is that ancient altar there," Elail continued, pointing with her tail fins, "and on it there is an engraving where the Rune of Life is intended to rest. If it sits in its spot, a protective life force will surround our courts and guard our gates, and all who dwell inside shall be saved from death! Only old age shall take us!"

Mangiat and Deiji frowned. "The Rune of Life belongs only to the Keeper of Life," Deiji said gently. "I am sorry, but your plan will not work. You should be secure in your numbers here to live peaceably enough, as no Ballas threaten you anymore."

"Silence!" Eligh roared. "Mermen!" A strong group of Mermen came from the cobbled halls and began to close around them menacingly. "Take them beyond the great walls and kill them."

"And the Pirates call them their friends," Mangiat muttered. "Can we not just leave?"

"I cannot let you leave and risk you stealing the Rune back from us." The Mermen showed their swords. He glanced at Deiji who appeared to be unafraid, and he felt his heart swell with pride at this.

"How did you know I would come?" she asked softly.

"Why must you know?" the Merman asked, folding his arms.

Deiji smiled blandly. "I only want to see where I went wrong, is all."

Eligh laughed. "It was very simple. Quite predictable, actually. What a girl wouldn't do for her great-grandfather!"

₪

THE BOY

Staring down the other side, Zechi could see trees, sparsely set. It wasn't as nearly as far down as he had just climbed, but it was just as steep. The voice called out again, "Someone! Help me! I'm here. Over here!" He could hear the sound of rushing water.

Zechi looked at the sheer drop to the ground and took a deep breath. There was a tree near enough to start, but it had only a few branches, all near the top. He wouldn't have the benefit of the trees' help this time, either. It would be all him. Well, this is what he trained for.

He stepped out into the air, palms forward, and he fell onto the nearest tree branch. He held on for a moment and dropped onto the next lowest branch. They were too far set apart to climb down one tree alone. He turned to the next tree and jumped, swinging from branch to branch, just as he had always practiced. But these trees were farther apart, and they were weaker, older. As he jumped to the next lowest tree, the bough he gripped with his fingers snapped under his weight. Zechi tumbled the rest of the way to the ground and rolled.

SMACK! He rolled into the tree's solid trunk with his face, and his nose felt numb beyond the pain. "Oh doe." He felt his face gingerly, but he already knew it was broken. He wiped his bloody hand on his pants and got to his feet.

He was standing on the edge of an abandoned rock quarry, a pit that was blocked from view by the trees. This part of Treehorn Island had been mined until it was exhausted.

Alongside the pit was one of the rivers, which ran through the little valley. On the far hill was a waterfall, the pool below it frothy and churning.

The river came in from the ocean, and he ran to it. He saw the orange tailfins of the Mermaid, the same whom Farlane had spoken to. He knew he must be close, and he slowed as he ran to the base of the waterfall.

"Bowat?" he shouted above the roar of the water.

"Here!" The voice was loud and clear now. Zechi leaned over the mouth of the river.

The Mermaid leapt out of the water, a sharpened shell in hand. She swiped at him with it, and he fell back in surprise.

"Zechi?"

He scrambled around at the voice, and found himself looking up into the reddened face of the Pirate Ruan. He was covered in moist dirt and bark from the climb down.

"Ruan? What..?"

"I seen yer climb away all sudden like after ye fought with the man Bowen, and I thought you mi' need help." He pointed one yellowed fingernail at the angry Mermaid who protected the waterfall. "Leave that one to me."

"How bid you get dowd here?" Zechi frowned up at the trees and the cliff face, holding his sleeve to his dripping nose.

Ruan grinned. "There's an old bucket path up the far side of the river bank," and he pointed to the curve of the cliff. "For water carriers."

Zechi began to laugh and he couldn't stop. After all that!

Without another word, Ruan kicked off his shoes and placed his jagged dagger between the remains of his teeth. He dove into the shallow water, and Zechi could see the struggle from above. He turned away. Mowat.

He waded into the river and stepped behind the falling sheets of water. There was a vast cavern here, and its floors dipped down into a large hole. Zechi scrambled down to it, sending wet rocks and pebbles scattering in all directions.

He peered down into the cone-shaped hole, which fanned out near its muddy bottom. "Bowat?" His nose throbbed painfully.

"I'm here!" the desperate voice cried out, and it broke into loud, gulping sobs of thankfulness. The mist and splatters of the waterfall had left the floor of the pit flooded, and the elderly man sat shivering in the pool of water. He was dressed in a crumpled blue robe, his hair and beard dirty and tangled. The wrinkles in his face were deep, and wet from the cave.

Zechi's heart went out to this man, whom he had never met. He had heard great tales of his power, heroic lore of this fantastic man who now lay weak and defeated, unable to even stand.

"Zechi." His voice was calm and relieved, as though Zechi's presence alone was the end of his sufferings. Somehow Mowat knew him, but his wonder at that did not matter. He needed help.

"I'b goig to get you out! It will only be a bobent, I swear it!" He cast about for a length of rope, but could find none. He heard Mowat moan and could not bear it. Finally, he turned his eyes to the sky and called for a friend with a shrill whistle.

"SCREECH!" Sure enough, the falcon appeared over the rise, swooped down through the waterfall and onto his outstretched arm. He fumbled about through one of his many pockets and produced a scrap of parchment and a quill.

"Have Mowat. Deep Forest. See you there. – Zechi."

"Gib this to Jai," he instructed as he tied it to Polk's leg. "And sed Geo! We hab got to get Bowat out ob here!"

ℿ

THE KEEPER OF FIRE

"My great-grandfather?" Deiji asked in disbelief. Her heart was pounding. Could this be true? She treaded water with her green tail as the Mermen gathered around them threateningly.

Eligh looked disappointed. "You did not know this?"

"No," she answered coldly. She looked sidelong at Mangiat, who looked back at her, aghast.

"Then why did you come?" The Merman looked surprised. Deiji did not answer.

"Well, you came to us anyhow!" Eligh said triumphantly. He pointed Deiji's curved sword at her. "My men may cause you harm without bringing any upon themselves – we are immortal now!"

"I need air," Arill interjected quietly.

"You have not gained what you believe you have." Deiji's voice was firm. She rummaged about in the bag she held on her belt beside her knife and presented the jar high into the water, pinched between her thumb and forefinger.

Eligh squinted at the thing. "What is it?"

"It is a Balla," she declared proudly. "If I open this jar, he will become a plague to you all."

Eligh waved one hand passively. "A small Balla is no threat, and besides, we are kept safe behind these walls."

"Bigger than Ahava," Deiji insisted, referring to the Mother of all Ballas, who she had killed five years earlier. Eligh paled a little.

"Father, perhaps we should listen to her," Elail suggested meekly, touching the pink sea star that swept back her hair.

"SILENCE!"

He stared at the jar skeptically. Deiji took a deep breath. "Puff, safely escort Mangiat and Arill to the shore of Treehorn Island right now. I will join you shortly."

"No!" Mangiat protested.

"No one has my leave to go!" Eligh cried, but the Dolphin and the Merman dissolved in a watery cloud. Deiji was alone now.

"I will open this," she insisted. "I know of your plan to flood the world. I will destroy you now, if I must."

"That you will not," Eligh growled.

Deiji reached for her knife quickly, grabbing it by the tip. She flicked it in his direction, and it spun through the water and stuck into his arm.

"Arrggh!" he yelled in pain, and his fellow Merpeople gasped and pointed as blood clouded the water.

"You do not have the stone. You are not immortal." She held up the little jar again and smiled. "It is your decision."

"Leave. Leave us now." He yanked the knife out and clutched his wounded arm.

"Give me my sword."

The Merman tossed it through the water and she caught it easily as it floated down. She held the jar out once again.

"Just one more thing. Where is Mowat?"

ﬡ

AUNT MICID

Micid Nun Cu was hiding behind a chunk of driftwood that lay on the dirty beach of Treehorn Island. The water was incessant as it poured its gray water onto the shore again and again, washing up rotten seaweed and dead fish. She stared down at the feathered remains of a gull that clung to the fringes of the shore and sighed impatiently.

A warrior she was not. The men were fighting, and from what she could see and hear when she dared to peek, they were easily winning. But several were wounded. A few fell.

A coward? Perhaps. But she knew her priority was her own neck. All would be well, so long as the Captain was alive at the end... She saw Deiji's falcon circling overhead, a piece of parchment on its leg. She scowled. She had always hated that bird.

It seemed to hover over the water for a time, circling high before spiraling low again, and she finally guessed that the filthy animal was waiting for Deiji. She rolled her eyes.

Many minutes passed and she was growing irritated at the sight of it and finally stood up.

Hesitating, she stuck one arm out awkwardly, and said, "come here, bird. I will give her your message." The falcon obediently swooped down onto her arm and she flinched, sickened by the feel of its cold, scaly talons. The claws dug into her arm sharply, leaving white marks on her skin. She hastily untied the note with her stubby fingers, then shouted more loudly than she intended to, "now go, will you!"

Polk flew up and away in the direction that he had come, back to the quarry. Micid stood on the shore for a while, feeling silly. She unraveled the note and read it.

"Have Mowat. Deep Forest. See you there. – Zechi."

She sat and pondered this a while, listening to the roar of the wind and waves. She rested upon a damp chunk of driftwood, the scrap of parchment fluttering in her fingertips.

When she heard a splash she found herself relieved. A Centaur emerged from the waves and Micid stood still, not daring to approach them. Several minutes dragged by and there came another movement from the water. It was Deiji.

"There you are!" Micid called out sourly.

"What is it?" Deiji asked with confidence, shaking water from her hair, and she shrank away. Micid was quite scared of her niece, and she held out the note soundlessly, withdrawing her hand as soon as she was able.

Deiji read it and thrust it into the hands of the Centaur who read it also, and she plunged back into the waves without a word. A few awkward minutes passed and she returned to the beach.

"Arill will meet us back in Nigh after we have done with the Deep Forest. With only the stream across now, he could only listen from the riverbank and will be useless. I must tend to something. Mangiat, find Zechi and go with him to the Deep Forest. See if you can join up before he leaves." The girl looked Micid right in the eyes, and she cringed.

"Thank you, Micid. And tell Captain Farlane I give my thanks as well. Tell him to come to the Nigh Bay when he has regrouped his men, and they have fully recovered. Nigh will reward them generously for what they have done." She bowed deeply, showing great respect.

Micid could only stare as the little cat lifted the girl high into the air until they were gone.

₪

THE KEEPER OF FIRE

Jai stood on the beach of Rainbow Reef, of the Trinity Islands. Her parents lived here on the fringes of the R and R villages. Not far off the coast, beneath the sea was the Mermaid Fortress they had just left. Travelling back and forth between the coasts of Nigh was getting to be exhausting.

She knew her parents lived on this beach, though she had not delivered them here herself – Mowat had. She had visited these waters before, but now that she thought of it, she had never actually set foot on the Islands themselves.

There was a large palm leaf hut on the beach up shore. She smiled. What a pleasant place for her parents to retire to after all their sufferings! The breeze was light and easy, the sea was very blue. It was clear overhead, and *so* sunny. It kissed the back of her legs and warmed them, and she found herself satisfied with the place.

She could see a blackened bonfire site on the beach, still smoldering after a late night fire. Deiji stepped into the doorway of the hut. It was simple, with three rooms, one larger than the others. She caught a glimpse of a macramé hammock in the side room, where the windows faced the ocean.

Wooden chairs and a low table sat off to the side of the large room, which also served as a kitchen. She frowned. The floors were also of wood.

"May I help you?" A slightly concerned, almost confused voice sounded from behind her. Deiji twisted around and saw her father, standing tall, his arms full of driftwood.

"Popo!" she cried out and he dropped the jumble of wood into the sand. She fell into his arms, surprised to find tears welling from her eyes and falling to her cheeks.

"Deiji?" Another voice. She broke away from her stunned father and saw her mother, J, emerge from the back room.

She was tall, and healthier than Deiji had ever seen her; her hair as dark and as long as her own. The sun had done her some good as well – her skin was bright and had a good healthy color.

Seeing all this goodness, she turned to her father, Kalano, who was smiling and proud. His hair was nearly to his shoulders, and dark as well. He seemed more rugged than she remembered, but happier, too.

She clasped her mother's hands. "Look at you!" J cried, and they all began to laugh.

"You have fared well?" Deiji asked them eagerly.

"Oh, yes!" J smiled. "The king still sends us Emeralds every month."

She did not let her smile falter, but she was shocked. She knew her parents had an allowance when they were moved, but she was surprised that Mangiat continued to care for her family in this way. She was touched, and nearly blurted out her news concerning the Centaur, but cut her words off. She wasn't ready.

"That is good," she said finally.

"Why have you come?" her mother asked mildly, and it struck Deiji that this was a legitimate question. It was true that she had not been to see her parents since her coronation.

"There is much happening in the world beyond, and I have need of your knowledge." They both looked so surprised and impressed that it made her uncomfortable.

"Shall we sit?" she suggested.

"Yes, yes! Please come in." J ushered them into the wooden chairs inside the main room and busied herself with mugs and liquid while Kalano and Deiji sat.

"Maia should be returning from the village soon," J said mildly.

Deiji's head snapped up. "Maia?"

"Yes, she is buying bread and a few other things. Don't tell me it's not only us you don't write letters to."

Deiji flinched at this rebuke, and glanced at her father as her mother handed her a cup of what she perceived to be coconut juice. Kalano grinned, and she knew it was mostly in jest. Before she could speak, a splash of red and green appeared in the doorway and Deiji was up and out of her chair before she realized what she was doing. "Maia!"

Her friend stared at her with large eyes. "Deiji..."

Deiji stepped forward to embrace her, taking in the tattered state of her once fine dress. As they parted from their hug, they both looked each other over.

She knew how she looked – strong and powerful and confident. What surprised her was how similar of an air Maia now carried. She last remembered her friend putting on quite a show of status and propriety that likely masked some inner fear. Yet here she was, her fine gown showing obvious signs of mending, and her usually composed face glowing with serenity.

"Maia! What are you doing here? Where is your husband?"

Maia smiled at her. "I came to stay with your parents for a time. They were always kind to me." She smiled down at where the pair still sat, and straightened her shoulders. "I have left my husband."

Surprised, Deiji nodded, sat down and motioned to a chair for Maia. "I am glad you are at home here, but why have you left your husband? I thought Par Jaque was a kind man."

"Kind he is indeed, but he has also made moral allowances that have to do with money." Maia sounded surprisingly bitter.

"He has joined the new wave of the slave trade?"

Maia nodded.

"I am proud of you, my friend." And she truly was. She had never seen her friend as radiant and self assured as she looked now.

"I am happy to wait on your parents here. I want no part in the path of Man on the mainland. The more I refuse to come home, the harder my husband works to secure a greater fortune," she added.

Deiji reached over and squeezed her hand. "Stay strong, friend."

"So why have you come?" Maia asked, returning her squeeze and letting go. It made her cringe a little that her presence must bear some greater significance to others, and it was even worse that they were right.

"I wanted to ask about our family," Deiji began, turning towards her parents.

They both paused and a glance passed between them before looking away. J placed a cup before Kalano and adjusted herself in her chair. She folded her hands together. "Our family."

"Yes." Deiji found herself serious. "Who was my great-grandfather?"

Her mother actually looked disappointed. Or was it relieved?

Maia stood and quickly busied herself in tidying up the cooking area. She carried a basket of dishes outside and disappeared.

"I'm sorry, my Juju," J began. "Our family heritage remains something of a mystery. My father told us nothing of my grandparents." She stood and took her husband's empty cup back to the wash basin.

"Well, do you know anything at all?" Deiji asked desperately, and her father smiled at her a little. "Tell me of my grandfather."

"Why, yes, you had a grandfather," J said brightly, bringing a bowl of red and purple berries to the table.

"What was he like?"

213

J frowned. "He was a restless soul, always quiet, as if plagued by some inner anger." Her eyes were distant, lost in this far off memory. "He was my father," she rasped quietly, as though to justify that claim. "But he left my mother very early on. He began to become disfigured – I think he was suffering from an ailment of some sort – my mother never really said. But he left before he took turn for the worse, and I never heard another thing of him."

"Ailment?" Deiji was intrigued. "What sort of ailment?"

"His skin became black, very black. And the tips of his fingers began to bleed..." J looked quite troubled now, and Deiji didn't want to push it, but her heart was racing.

"Ma," she began slowly, "what was his name?"

"Oh, I don't even know why I said that." J looked flustered and stood to smooth her skirt. She took up the broom and began to sweep feverishly.

"What was his name?" Deiji repeated sharply, tears stinging the corners of her eyes. She stood up.

Her mother looked up, her face twisted in pain.

"Relant."

Deiji sat down again, very hard.

ת

"I have to go." Deiji's head was spinning. This was too much! Mowat *and* Relant? But it all made perfect sense...

"Deiji..." J looked over at her with large, dark eyes.

"I'm sorry." She meant it. "I love you both. Thank you for telling me this." She walked out the door and onto the bright beach.

"Puff Puff!" The cat appeared next to the fire pit, waiting. "Winged horse."

Puff began her transformation into a large, white winged Pegasus and Deiji leapt onto her back.

Maia came around the corner and stood beside J. They watched quietly as she steered her horse towards the open horizon.

"Jai!" It was her father, standing in the sand. She turned back to him.

"You... You have the most beautiful green eyes," he said fondly.

Deiji grinned and they turned towards the sky.

₪

THE KING

"We bust go to the Deep Forest," Zechi insisted, whistling shrilly with his fingers for the Dragon. "Oi! Geo!"

"Wait, Zechi," Mangiat said sternly. He was afraid. Things looked bleak. Where was Jai? She didn't say where she had gone to! If they were to battle in the Deep Forest, they would be without her help.

"Sir, we bust go, and soon!"

Geo appeared overhead, flying down from the quarry at Zechi's call. Mowat was clinging to his back.

215

"Geo! Mowat!" Mangiat cried out to him as he landed softly. "We must go to the Nigh Court! Can you..." He gulped. "Can you carry me?"

Geo nodded his scaly head. Zechi clambered across Geo's back – the boy could ride anything! – behind Mowat, and they rose into the air.

"Zechi, see to Mowat," he instructed. "Make sure he is okay for the journey."

Geo hovered over Mangiat and closed his talons gently over his midsection. They were under way.

₪

It was hours before the familiar view of the castle was clear beneath his windmilling hooves. "Drop us in the court, Geo!" he called up. "Well, not *drop*," he added as an afterthought. There was the definite sensation of falling as Geo folded his wings and plummeted towards the castle.

"Please... gently. Oh, please." He closed his eyes and breathed. He did not like the ground rushing up so quickly at him. How unnatural this was! He moved his hooves as though to run as the ground swiftly approached.

Geo slowed and set him lightly upon the grass, letting go at the last possible second. Mangiat stumbled, then found his footing. The Dragon landed nearby.

"What do we do?"

Mangiat was sweaty, stressed and tired, but Zechi appeared to be more than ready to go. He looked into his student's large brown eyes and saw a serious soul. It was time.

"I will round up the men in the surrounding army encampments. I need you to head to the Nigh stables and prepare the horses."

Zechi raised his eyebrows. "All of theb?"

"All of them."

The boy gave a curt nod and began to jog towards the castle.

"Zechi!" Mangiat called out, "that is not the way to the stables!"

"I doe!" he called back without looking. "I deed bore knives; I hab lost bine!"

Mangiat smiled and looked at Geo. Mowat was on his back in something of a restful trance. He looked exhausted. "Geo, you're with me. We may be compelled to use brute force in this venture."

ᛡ

THE BOY

His broken nose was smarting.

Within an hour he had nearly twenty horses groomed and bridled. Leaning toward the ground as he cleaned out their hooves brought a great deal of pressure to his nose, and he wanted to finish the job as quickly as he was able.

He had led them out of the corral one by one and tied them to the rail that ran beside the path. Each one was brushed down, its hooves cleaned out, and bridled before being tied to the rail to await its saddle and rider. The horses shifted around restlessly, some attempting to drop their heads to graze.

He was cleaning out one black mare's hooves when Men began to pour into the stable yard. Soldiers began to take up his work, fetching and tying the remaining horses, some saddling up and mounting the waiting ones. The Centaurs and Elvin soldiers stood huddled together on the side, waiting.

Mangiat appeared in the dooryard looking fierce. "We will need weapons," he said simply, and Zechi nodded. He handed the hoof pick to a nearby solider and walked to the cellar doors, then threw them open.

"Help yourselbs, ben."

He stood back and there was a steady stream of soldiers in and out. They reappeared with swords and knives alike, each armed with a crossbow. The men slowly returned to their horses. Zechi noticed that any interactions between the three races were wholly negative – some shoved each other out of the way, swore, or gnashed their teeth.

"We will assemble in the courtyard!" Mangiat announced above the din, and Zechi was surprised to hear the men grumble. He looked into their weathered faces and saw that many men were reluctant and irritated. He ran ahead to the courtyard with Mangiat. Mowat was still perched upon Geo. He looked exhausted, but still keen to know what was happening.

"Do they not want to fight?" Zechi inquired quietly as he jogged to keep up with the Centaur.

"No," the king answered coldly. "They do not see a cause here. As far as they are concerned, this world can fall apart at their hooves or feet and they will only rejoice in it. If it were not for Geo's teeth, they would not be here."

"A cause? They do not see a cause? Ibpossible."

Mangiat stood beside the podium in the courtyard and Zechi joined him as the men and their officers lined up astride their horses. Geo and Mowat flew overhead, waiting for instructions.

The men's agitation seemed to spread to their horses, for they shifted about and made to turn as if to go. The soldiers continually straightened their horses back around and tried to focus on their king.

Mangiat cleared his throat. "Men, we ride into the Deep Forest," he announced. "There we will find those responsible for the illegal deforestation of the sacred wood. This new trade that fuels the slavery of the Elves is due to the overproduction of jewels to meet the demand."

The men began to mutter amongst themselves and Zechi even saw a few yawn. He lost his temper, his blood boiling with impatience and rage.

"Listen, fools!" he cried, leaping to the top of the podium and knocking Mangiat out of the way. The king did not rebuke him, so although he waited for chastisement, he plowed on.

"Soldiers of Nigh! Stop what you are doig!" He felt foolish, but all the men and their horses stared at him, their ears alert. He cleared his throat.

"There is no deed to resist as you do! We hab one hundred soldiers here, some Ben, some Centaur and Elf. Does it batter? Your duty is to protect Nigh. Hab you forgotten?"

219

"Sir!" a soldier, a Man called out from the crowd. "Sir, we will not fight to save those we despise, Sir!"

"Why do you dot watch your brethren's backs in battle?" Zechi countered. "What is the difference between a Ban and a Bystic? No bore segregation!" He thumped his fist upon the podium. "Do dot fool yourselbs into thinking the world will rebain this way. *There will be change.* There is buch bore at stake besides the petty squabbling of peasants who cannot bear to lives abongst each other! Let it go!"

He was livid now, his bloody nostrils flaring painfully. The crowd was silent. "Jai has a plan to sabe you all. You will not hab to bear it buch longer, but we bust do our part. Go, will you! We ride dorth to the Deep Forest. Protect our world, ben."

He glanced at Mangiat as the men cheered. To his relief, his Teacher looked impressed. "How did you know that Deiji has a plan?" he asked.

Zechi grinned. "It's *Jai*, Bangiat! Of course she has a plan." He jumped off the platform and mounted the nearest standing horse. The men roared and applauded as Zechi led the way north.

Mowat looked down at Mangiat. "He is a good choice," Zechi heard him say approvingly, and his ears were red as he pretended not to notice Mowat's words.

ꄍ

The Calvary arrived to the south of the part of the Deep Forest that was being logged. When they glimpsed the men at work with their axes, Zechi cried out at the extent of the damage.

Already a full acre had been cleared for the men's campsite, and it was littered with their supplies and belongings. Another two acres had been cleared out, and it was their worksite. Seeing the cut tree stumps and fallen trees filled Zechi with such a rage and disgust that he could wait no longer. He leapt from his horse and joined Mowat on Geo's back. They rose above the trees.

"I take by leabe here, men! Geo, take Bowat to…" He paused as his men poured into the forest. Would the Nigh court be safe? "To the Odel billagers! Bowat, tell theb you are Jai's friend, and you are in need. They will care for you until we send for your return. Cobe back ibbediately, Geo!"

He slid from Geo's back into the trees without waiting for a response, or waiting for Geo to stop. He fell through the air, caught a branch roughly and clung there. Something was sticky on his hands. He pulled them away, clinging to the tree with his thighs. Tree sap. The trees were bleeding.

As he hung so, he spoke a brief message to Sounet, pressing his palms meaningfully upon its trunk. "By dear friend, I hab returned to the trees! Stay with be, for there is buch at stake. Gib be branches!"

"My sisters are in pain, my friend!" Sounet uttered quietly. A bough lifted for him and he reached for it as he jumped and swung his way to the clearing of men.

There he crouched among the treetops and watched these men work below him. He listened to

221

their words. His heart leapt with burning anger when he saw General Morim strolling through the campsite, clutching the royal scepter tightly as he was flanked by Gance and Nia.

"Soon there will be more jewels to fuel the industry, my lord," Gance said slyly.

"And you will, no doubt, keep a handful to yourself," Morim muttered. Gance's expression did not falter, and Nia's smile grew wider on her thin lips.

"We shall double our quota. Two acres per day will keep this investment at a prime," she announced. The General looked surprised. Zechi knew the Mystical creatures would not stand for it.

"And why do we make such an increase? I thought the idea was to avoid war."

"Well, my lord, we are doing away with such Mystical creatures as would fight against us. They will be forced the Lost Marshes and can say no more. We will even expand our camps up and down the forest so that Nigh can take what it needs."

"The next three years will be fruitful," Gance added.

"Will there even be a forest in three years?" Morim asked plainly.

The Elf answered coolly, "does it matter?"

Zechi could stand to hear no more. He let out an angry growl at this, and he shouted, "Trees – REBEL! Men, CHARGE!"

The men came tearing through the trees on their mounts, swinging their swords and discharging their crossbows. Zechi released his hold and fell into the clearing, right at the General's feet! Morim looked shocked, to say the least, and Zechi had to grin in spite of his anger.

The trees began to move, swinging their branches at the men who cut them down, attacking them, swatting at them like flies. Some wrapped their vines around men's legs or necks, and hurled them off into the distance, outside of the camp.

Zechi stood tall before his tutor and stared him down. "How dare you do what you hab done," he hissed coldly through his broken nose, and he was surprised when Morim actually looked ashamed.

The cries of Men filled the air as the trees fought back. They were joined by the Calvary of Men and the free standing Centaurs who plowed through the groups of men quickly. Everywhere Zechi could hear the sounds of pounding hooves and the loggers' terrified shouts.

He knew with Jayna being gone that the trees would have waited for the command to fight back – even to death. But the trees listened to him. They always listened to him.

The General's downcast eyes fell upon the jeweled scepter he gripped in his hand as the battle raged around him. His fingers loosened, and it fell to the forest floor with a thud.

Zechi picked it up thoughtfully, turning it over in his hands. He looked at the General, then swung it like a club, knocking him out cold.

נ

THE KING

Mangiat was filled with excitement as he arrived at the battle in the Deep Forest. The trees were violently tearing into their aggressors, the Calvary had taken the forest, and he was ready to join the fight. It was time to defend his home. He leapt into the battle with only one thought, swinging his short sword at the loggers and tree cutters.

"Out! Out of my forest!"

Some men fought. Most ran, afraid of the trees, which seemed to have taken on a life of their own. Mangiat laughed as he turned upon a round of men to fight. His eyes fell past them, upon a boy dressed in the peasant's garb that he always found so comfortable. He was holding the king's scepter, and for a moment Mangiat was confused.

Then... "You meddlesome boy!" It was the shrill voice of Nia, who, with one sharp movement, withdrew from her cane a slender sword. Zechi blocked it easily with the scepter, which dented, being made of gold, and he backed away – right into the hands of Gance.

"Slit his throat!" the woman yelled, and Gance produced his knife. Mangiat made to move, but found himself faced against men, many men... More soldiers of Bowen had arrived, some fifty of them. They wore the gray soldier's garb, and their boots were black. He was thankful that most of them had remained on Treehorn Island for the time, although it was plain that this was going to turn ugly.

His heart was flooded in fear for the boy who he quite nearly called son, and of the men that stood between them. Where was Deiji?

224

"Stop!" a voice came down from the heavens. But it was not Jai.

Docin flew down astride River, who wrapped her scaly blue talons around Gance's shoulders. He slashed at her aimlessly, then froze, paralyzed, releasing the boy.

"Drop the knife," Docin commanded. "You make any other movement than I command and my Dragon makes a market fish out of you."

"The battle continues!" someone cried.

"Do not worry – the soldiers of Nigh ride after them!" Zechi called out.

Gance's eyes were wide, but Mangiat did not see what happened next. The men were nearing him with their long swords, and he raised his own to fight them, wary of the outcome of such odds. A quick glance behind them, and he realized...

"Wait! Where is Nia? Where did Nia go?" Mangiat cried in the confusion.

Then out of the brush a misty barrier rose around him, almost like a shield. He could see the faint face of a little cat floating inside it, and he grinned. "Puff Puff!"

"Hold fast, king! My master comes to save you!"

Sure enough, Jai appeared before them, facing the men with her silver sword that was dripping with the blood of others. Where she had been he did not know, but she had certainly worked to save them! She stood tall, powerful in her white sari, and her eyes burned a deep green.

"Take your leave or your lives are forfeit," she growled at the men, and they made haste to run away.

225

"Thank you, Jai."

She nodded and turned away. "I must see to Mowat," she said urgently, looking around at all of them.

"Geo has taken hib to the Odel Billage," Zechi volunteered, and Deiji gave a curt nod. She and Puff Puff disappeared.

Mangiat turned to Zechi, who was surveying the damage to the woods. The fight had subsided and all was eerily quiet. River gazed at the sky quietly, looking for Geo, no doubt.

The Dragon Keeper tied Gance to a tree a few yards away, and Mangiat laughed, and he turned to thank Docin. Then…

"FOOL!" A flash of silver and Nia leapt from the brush, landing on Docin, who tumbled over into the dirt, the woman falling with him. Mangiat rushed to his side and pulled her away, restraining her, but it was too late.

Docin looked shocked where he lay, his eyes wide and bulging. Nia's knife was stuck deep into his chest.

רו

He thrust the Elder Nia against a tree, and vines snapped forth and held her captive alongside Gance. Mangiat fell to Docin's side and knew right away there was nothing to be done for the man.

The Dragon Keeper lay gasping, his hand on his Dragon for comfort. Zechi crouched over the fallen man, whose white face was impossibly pale. Docin opened his mouth to speak, focusing his blue eyes on River.

"My dear friend," he panted, "find your way to Geo. Stay with him. I… I wish you so much happiness!" He began to sob as much as he was able. River lowered her blue face to her Master and closed her eyes mournfully.

The man sought out the face of Zechi, and Mangiat found himself holding back some tears. He coughed a little and looked away to save himself.

"Tell Deiji… Tell her I am sorry for trying to steal the Rune." A tear ran down his dry and dirty face, from his eye to his ear. "Tell her that, lad." He began to shiver.

"I bill." Zechi nodded earnestly. "I bill." And he held the man's hand until he was gone.

ℶ

THE DRAGON

Geo returned from Mount Odel in hopes to fight in the battle. What he saw, however, was not what he expected.

The clearing was quiet, the men were gone. Zechi and River were crouched over a fallen man, and Mangiat stood off to the side. He knew something was wrong.

Geo landed nearby and River turned to him. They crossed necks and stood together a moment. She leaned into him heavily, and over her shoulder Geo could see that Docin was dead.

Nia and Gance were tied to a tree behind him, and Geo growled, understanding and angered. Mangiat cleared his throat.

"There will be a proper trial and judgment to be passed on these two, my friend. Do not take your vengeance now, for you will witness it later among the whole of Nigh."

Geo nodded.

"Will you help me carry these back to the Nigh courts for such a trial?" he asked River respectfully.

The Dragon nodded, pride and sadness written clearly across her slender face. Mangiat nudged another body with his hoof. "We should take Morim, too. I think he is still alive. And Docin, who deserves a hero's burial."

Geo moved forward to help his mate, but Zechi called out, "doe, and wait a while, Geo. There is one last thing we bust do."

River accepted these two across her back, and took Gance and Nia in her talons. She rose into the air slowly and left for Nigh. Mangiat gave the promise that he would meet her there.

After she had gone, Geo looked at Mangiat, who looked at Zechi.

"Follow be," the boy said, his nose now dripping a dark blood, which he continually wiped away from his chaffed upper lip with his soiled sleeve. They began to walk through the woods. It wasn't long until they came to a familiar spot among the trees.

It was a small clearing, and the sun shone in lightly. Butterflies floated across the path and Fairies flitted about quickly. The sweet chatter of birds was abundant, and they looked to the place where Jayna once stood. It seemed too pleasant a place for such a grave. The spot was still charred and burned out. All that remained was a blackened stump.

Both Mangiat and Zechi fell to their knees in reverence, and Geo watched them respectfully, wondering if he would catch up to River and share her burdens.

"I have not been to see it," Mangiat whispered, and Zechi nodded.

"Nor hab I." He stood and took his bag of Sapphires and newly added Emeralds from his neck and poured them into his palm. He picked out the Emeralds and added a single Sapphire to the pile. Geo watched this, curious, as the boy leaned over the stump and let them spill from his fingers. They plinked against one another and twinkled in the early evening's light. Geo looked at Mangiat who shrugged, but still seemed interested.

"Geo," the boy said with a passion, "breathe your green bagic upon her!"

Understanding, he obediently moved forward and opened his mouth. He blew a bright green crackling flame upon the charred wood, then stood back, holding his breath, hoping… The flame caught onto the coals of the stump, setting it alight, and it spread quickly.

Then, little green shoots began to pop up from around the stump. Fresh wood began to grow hurriedly, and it twisted itself up into the form of a woman, right before their eyes. Her features appeared to be carved out of oak, and her expression was one of great beauty and sadness. But there was also something greater in her eyes, Geo thought with admiration. Something fantastic was here. It was hope.

Vines began to grow from her head and they trailed to the ground. She smiled at them. Mangiat was crying.

"Go, my children, repair the damage to my forest." Her voice was sweet.

Geo stood proud as Zechi laughed and Mangiat cried out in exhilaration through his tears.

The Queen of the Forest had been reborn.

Chapter Twelve
The Water

THE KEEPER OF LIFE

*D*eiji arrived at the Nigh Village somewhat
sheepishly. The locals she had known her entire
peasant life now revered her so carefully, she
knew… She found discomfort in such attention, and
always had.

Sure enough, as she walked into the village,
people began to shout and drop what they carried.
Children ran to the huts of their parents, and woman
shrieked from their doorsteps, "she is come! She is
come!"

"She is looking for her friend!"

"Let us bring her to him!"

"Follow us!"

She found herself caught up in a gaggle of loud
children. She was uncomfortable in their presence,

as if she might trod upon their small bodies, or corrupt their little minds.

Jai allowed herself to be led up the village path to the Baker's hut. How strange it all seemed! Now that she had taken the time to look, these paths which she had grown up on were now so odd and simple. It was smaller than she remembered.

Pav the Baker greeted her at the threshold. She was a round woman, her face, apron and even her graying hair streaked with the flour of her countertops. She had a very full jaw, and it quivered as her speech ran on, a constant dribble that never stemmed itself.

"Come in, come in!" She bowed deeply. "Your elderly friend rests in my bedchamber. He is ill, ah, he is famished! Bread and water I have given him, and do you desire any yourself? He is a polite thing, he is!"

Deiji actually laughed at Pav's ramblings. Well, one thing had not changed!

"You must come and stay a spell, and tell me all of the world beyond. What a thing it is indeed, to have such a wench from this very village to go off and become more than –"

"Pav." She held up one hand. "Please show me in to him."

"Right away! Right away!" The robust woman brushed flour from her hands, and led Deiji behind the stoves, into the two rooms of her private dwelling.

Mowat lay upon the bed, looking so weak and frail that it brought tears to her eyes. Rain pattered on the roof outside, and Jai knelt at his side, taking his hand. She looked up at Pav.

"Leave us." The woman disappeared.

His hair and beard were whiter than snow, and the wrinkles in his face were deeply set, showing his age. He was thinner than she remembered, and he shivered in his thin blue robes.

Jai looked him over carefully, her eyes welling with tears. He seemed very near his end. She closed her eyes and whispered, *"Hertzel."* She opened them to see Mowat's body renew itself, clean, smooth flesh overtaking his face and hands. She closed her eyes again and took him to her space.

They stood among the stars and she was relieved when she saw him looking at her with pride, wearing a fresh linen robe.

"You came for me."

"You are my friend and my Teacher. How could I not?"

He smiled. "You have a question."

"You have something to tell me," she countered. "You can now tell me that which was burning so brightly inside you to possess you to cross the Southern Ocean by rowboat." Her tone was teasing, her green eyes sparkling like the stars around them.

"How is Arill?" he asked brightly.

"He is well," she answered, and was pleased when he smiled. "He waits for you in the Bay outside the Nigh castle," she added. He nodded.

She continued, "The Merpeople tell me that we are of a relation, you and I."

Mowat sighed and smiled. "It is true. This is what I had to tell you, before I lost it all and became nothing more than an old man. My child, you are my great-granddaughter. And I came to say that I am *very* proud of you, as I will die soon."

She sidestepped his last statement, unwilling to speak of such a thing.

"So you are my…"

"Your mother's father's father. Yes, I am Relant's father," he supplied. "That is why your heritage and abilities are so rich with magic."

"I heard about Relant, too." She looked down at her bare feet and the stars beneath them.

"Yes, I thought you might learn of that."

"Why did you not tell me sooner?" She looked him in the eye again.

"Jai, mine is a sad story. Jayna and I lost our connection with our child many years ago. I had an inkling that I had found your mother, my granddaughter, only she was ill… Then I discovered she had a daughter. I sought you out. Only when you sat upon the throne of Nigh and declined it did I know the truth."

"How did that reveal such a truth?" She needed to know.

He laughed. "Because you are so much like myself!" His eyes flashed green. "I would never take a throne for myself while the whole world waited for me. And I wanted to tell you this before it was too late. As you have grown stronger with your title, I grow weaker. I wanted you to know the truth."

"It is an amazing truth, Mowat. And do you know that Jayna was killed? And that I can see that Geo has rebirthed her under Zechi's direction?"

234

"I am relieved," Mowat admitted. "Jayna and I have shared a real but distant love for most of our lives. I have always intended to return to her side when I retire and spend the rest of our lives in love, but I was afraid I missed my chance. Now I see a second chance and I want to take it."

Deiji smiled, thinking of Mangiat. "We will make it happen," she promised.

"I am truly thrilled." Mowat's smile was as large as she had ever seen it. "Please forgive me for not telling you of our relation sooner. There have been many deathbed confessions on my mind as of late. Yours was at the top of my list. I need to finish it."

She raised her eyebrows. "We must make that happen also, then."

"You are truly ready to take over my post as the Keeper of Life, Teacher of life, the Necromancer." He motioned to all the galaxies and myriad of planets in the space around them. "There are so many worlds, so many beings that need guidance." He seemed a little sad, and she knew that letting all this go, all these worlds he had influenced and governed for hundreds of years was difficult for him.

She placed a hand on his shoulder. "Thank you. But what about here? What of the world of Nigh and its problems? What do I do next? I know this is not over."

"You know what to do, Jai. You always have."

She looked up at his old, wizened face. He had seen so much in his time! She nodded, accepting this. "I know I do."

"You are truly my descendant."

They stood together there, saying no more, and watched the sun rise over the edge of a distant world.

₪

THE KING

Who ever knows what these things can bring? After all this, Mowat is sound, Jai and I are together – and I can scarcely write those words and call them truth!

There is one last thing we must do, one thing to resolve all these problems between Man and Mystical... and I am sure it will bring all to a peaceful end...

Three days later Mangiat looked up from his journal in the courts of Nigh, breathing satisfaction. Last night the stars had shown him wonderful, sure things to come. Morim, Gance and Nia waited in the Nigh prison, the verdict being a strict one.

General Morim had cooperated, giving Mangiat a full account of his actions. The king was reluctant, but punishment was to be had, nonetheless. Morim was to stay on, in servitude to the throne till the end of his life. He would be eternally cut off from his origins, cut off from the sea.

Nia would be sent along with everyone else, and with all the prisoners. It would be up to the new society to punish her justly. Gance had gotten what he wanted, however, even if it was different than he

236

had anticipated. Man and Mystic would be separated at last. Or, rather, joined.

The Elf was sent back into his own people's settlement for judgment, and Mangiat knew he would hear from the man no longer, the Elvin race being what it was. So these two were afraid.

Docin had a proper and honorable funeral at dawn, and even the Pirates attended, uncomfortable as they were. River and Geo had stood there reverently, honoring what he was to them, and basking in his memory. They were a pair now, and would stay together. But Geo would always be there when Deiji needed him... Always.

The Deep Forest had been renewed, thanks to Geo and Zechi. Jayna was reborn from the ashes and took her place as Queen of the Forest once more. Jai had even mended Zechi's broken nose.

They stood in the bay of Nigh once more, staring out into the water where Arill swam impatiently among one hundred Merpeople. All of Nigh's Men had been summoned from every town and village, and most of the Mystical people had been invited to witness the spectacle.

Thousands of them milled about: Centaurs of all colors; Elves and Pegasus; Rabbits hopped about at their feet. Fairies fluttered about around the heads of a few reluctant Dwarves. Among them stood the sentenced people – the men, women and children of Nigh.

Mangiat thought with a hollow sadness of the huts and shops across Nigh that sat empty now... The livestock had been set free, and they brought an end to monies and trade. It would be better, he decided.

He watched as Deiji knelt at the waterline and spoke with Eligh and other Merpeople he had brought with him. Mowat stood beside her, proud to see her doing what she was meant to do in this life. He came close into the water without hesitation, even wading up to his knees to hear them speak.

"Mowat once told me that the whole sea would not soon forget what I had done for you," she was saying. "Five years ago I helped you to defeat a creature that threatened your lives every day, a creature that kept your families from joining together. You once made the decision to send half of your people ashore, so as to guarantee your numbers. You did this in an act of pure hope. Your world is secure now, and the preserved numbers are ready to be added. It is time for them to return."

Mangiat walked away. This was an incredible day in Nigh history.

He saw Zechi, sitting astride a black horse he had claimed from his abandoned village. He was still holding the scepter. Mangiat knew right then that Zechi would be, *must* be, exempt. Mowat and Deiji came over to where he stood staring.

"What will you do now?" Mangiat asked the elderly man.

"I do not know." An unlikely answer. Mowat looked at Jai, who smiled.

"You and Jayna might deserve some time together," she suggested.

"Yes, yes. We have been waiting for many, many years to be together. And I need to see to Arill as well. I have that which I need to tell him. An apology that is due before I pass on." They looked out at the bay where Arill breached, frustrated and eager to be part of the action.

"Where shall I send you?" she asked. Mangiat was curious to hear Mowat's answer.

"To the stars." The man's face was still fixed upon his Dolphin companion.

"Then you shall go. And to Jayna after." Deiji closed her eyes and bowed her head. A soft silver light began to wrap around the man's body, and he was lifted into the air. Mangiat watched, fascinated, as Mowat faded, then disappeared. A quick look to the bay confirmed Arill's absence as well.

She smiled at Mangiat, and he took her hand.

"Well, here we are." The girl took a deep breath. "It is the day."

"Jai, I wanted to discuss Zechi."

"Mm? Oh, yes, I will definitely be taking him on as my student after this."

"There is more to it. After his training under you, I believe I will pass on the duties of governing the throne to the boy. Even without Man, the Mystical peoples will need some leadership... And I don't believe Zechi would fare well away from the trees."

"You would make him king?" she asked incredulously. He felt triumph. There was one thing she had not thought of!

"Yes."

She smiled. "It is good."

They both looked sidelong at the boy, who was watching the masses of Man gather on the shore before him and his horse. He seemed calm, tranquil, as if he had finally achieved some destiny of his own.

"Then what will you do?"

He grinned. "I will care for the throne until Zechi is ready. Then I shall return to the Deep Forest and help Jayna as I always have. Maybe offer counsel to Zechi when he is need of it." He looked down shyly. "And I want to stay with you. What of yourself?"

She laughed. "I will be here for you. With you. But there are other worlds that need tending to."

They looked out upon the lines of men, women and children who waited on the edge of the bay. Micid had stood in tears that morning, frightencd of this new place where she was now compelled to go. Captain Farlane motioned her to come to his side, and she moved eagerly to him. Even the Pirates were to return to the sea, and they stood there excitedly, hands hovering over their swords, led by Ruan. To them this was just another great adventure. J and Kalano stood nearby, waiting.

The Captain was to stay in the Nigh castle, where it was decided he would take Morim's place. After all, Farlane was an educated man, and had lived among the people long enough to know the world for what it was.

He refused, time and again to share his story, but Mangiat was sure that Zechi would pry it from him bit by bit. He smiled at the thought. Micid stepped up beside Farlane, and she stuttered her thanks. They were to stay, in servitude to the throne, for all time. Some of the only remainder of Man.

"I think it is time." Mangiat stepped up onto a large rock that sat very nearly in the water itself. The waves lapped about half of it, but he was no longer afraid.

"Citizens of Nigh!" The murmuring crowd fell silent as he shouted, and they all looked to him.

"Over five years ago you discovered the truth of Mystical presences in this world. And further, you found out that you were once of a blood! I stand here to tell you to go. Return to the water that gave you birth. It is time for you to go home. It is time!"

He raised his arms into the air and watched Geo and River circling the bay overhead, happy together. They would join with their kin, taking the forest, the rivers, the mountains for their own as it once was. He grinned and stepped back. He took Deiji's hand and they watched, together.

"Where will they go, Jai?"

"The Mermaid Fortress, most likely. They will lose their legs and gain their fins once they submerge," she explained.

Thousands of Man faced the sea and began to walk, some hesitating, some plunging in quickly, eager to see their new world.

He felt a tug on his arm, and Jai was rising into the air, pulling him with her. They hovered above the people as they moved into the water, row after row.

He looked at his beautiful spouse. It was the beginning to her reign over the Universe. A beautiful white light surrounded her, growing larger then bursting, sending itself out to every corner of the horizon.

241

Zechi was leaning over the water, a tinkling cascade of Sapphires slipping from his pouch and into the bay.

Jai lifted her hands and cried, *"Wandeln Sie Um!"*

Transform...

The End

About The Author

Davina Liberty (yes, that's her real name!) lives on the largest of the San Juan Islands, Orcas Island.

She works as a Marine Naturalist on a whale-watching boat encouraging responsible viewing and providing educational talks, primarily on orca whales.

When she's not working she rides her horses, freedives and travels internationally.

Coming Soon!

Take a sneak peek into the third and final installment of the Dolphin Code!

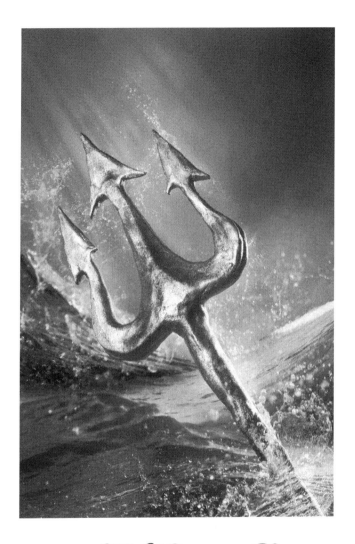

The Mermaid's Plight
**Book Three of
the Dolphin Code Trilogy**

246

Kani the wolf was bounding across the cave floor calling out for the Teacher, his shaggy tail hanging low behind him as he loped across the stars.

"Mowat!"

A thin blue light cut through the stars of the cave's ceiling and the shadowy figure of a man appeared through the haze. Kani waited patiently as the form came into focus. A wizened elder in robes of blue hovered before him.

"I was overseeing the distant earth of Man," Mowat explained. "The Humans there have grown to extreme numbers and can no longer sustain life on their planet if they continue to breed at such a rate. I have a few ideas to submit to their Keepers for better management. Now, what requires my attention?" he asked, not unkindly.

Kani smiled, baring his white fangs. "I apologize for interrupting your work," he said hastily. "I have just come from scouting the near earth called Nigh. One of the dominant species there are struggling with just the opposite issue and I can foresee the eventual loss of their species."

"Which species?"

"The Merpeople. There is an abundance of predators that is killing them faster than they can breed. The Dolphins and Whales are also in danger, but the Merpeople are more immediately threatened."

"There are no Keepers there," Mowat said slowly. "We haven't established anything there yet, and to do so would require a full exploration. What do you advise?"

Kani sighed. "From what I can tell, Merpeople are naturally skeptical of strangers. I do not think you could go as you are and Teach them. Additionally, they have a fear of non-Mer magic. It was quite complex for me to blend in as a stranger. Their communities are so small they all seem to know and recognize each other."

"This does present a problem," Mowat agreed. "It would do little good to spend my time there earning their allegiance. If one thing goes wrong then I will lose all ground."

"Then I suggest we turn the scales. Turn back thirty-five years and be born there. Grow up among them and you will be a trusted member of the population. You will also learn enough to discover how to solve this."

Mowat nodded. "Brilliant. I shall be born a Merman. I will retain my ability to become Man again on land; that is important."

"You will also locate and establish Keepers over at least four Elements of Nigh. We must have those to follow on after you depart."

The pair walked across the vast emptiness of space, Mowat's blue light leaving echoing traces behind them. Mowat called forth the Hourglass of Time and tilted it, muttering an incantation for thirty-five years. He smiled at the wolf.

"I will see you from time to time on the shore, my friend."

"Indeed. Enjoy the life, my master. And Mowat?"

"Yes?" Mowat halted before finishing the tilt.

"Remember that you are not truly a part of this life. Last time you got a little too close. Do not make the same mistake again."

Mowat nodded grimly, not meeting Kani's eyes as he placed the hourglass on its opposite end. There was a flash of blue and he was gone.

Made in the USA
Middletown, DE
22 December 2021

56847733R00151